D0838030

Also by Bill Naughton in Panther Books

Late Night on Watling Street
One Small Boy
Alfie Darling

Bill Naughton

Alfie

PANTHER
GRANADA PUBLISHING
London Toronto Sydney New York

Published by Granada Publishing Limited
in Panther Books 1966
Reprinted 1966 (seven times), 1967 (twice), 1968,
1969 (twice), 1971 (twice), 1972, 1973, 1977

ISBN 0 586 02805 6

First published by MacGibbon & Kee Ltd 1966
Copyright © Bill Naughton 1966

Granada Publishing Limited
Frogmore, St Albans, Herts AL2 2NF
and
3 Upper James Street, London W1R 4BP
1221 Avenue of the Americas, New York, NY10020 USA
117 York Street, Sydney, NSW 2000 Australia
100 Skyway Avenue, Toronto, Ontario, Canada M9W 3A6
Trio City, Coventry Street, Johannesburg 2001, South Africa
CML Centre, Queen & Wyndham, Auckland 1, New Zealand

Made and printed in Great Britain by
C. Nicholls & Company Ltd
The Philips Park Press, Manchester
Set in Monotype Baskerville

Contents

BOOK ONE

"Money is everything"

CHAPTER ONE

"ALFIE," she said, "are you starting all over again?"
It was Siddie, my regular Thursday night bint, a married woman of twenty-nine, so she said, but she could be thirty-two or three, or even thirty-five topweight, and quite a fair bit of grumble, clean as a nut, a trifle on the leggy side for my fancy, with muscles on her calves, but she's got this beautiful chest, and she's a handsome dresser, and a good speaker. In fact, a woman you can take anywhere, so what more do you want for three or maybe four vodka-and-tomato juices once a week, and every other round she stands her corner into the bargain, slipping the money to me under the table.

"What about it if I am?" I said.

Know what, she's only putting the idea into my mind, hoping it'll take root. I mean I've no idea of starting anything until I hear her mention it. We'd had it off on the back seat, see, stripped down a bit for the job, and when we've done I get out to water the old geranium against the offside rear wheel – (I've been pinting it, see) and generally unjangle myself, and then I put on my jacket and slip in front into the driver's seat, not forgetting to give her a last cuddle just to show I done it all out of love, and not lust, when blow me down if she ain't inciting me all over again. Well, in for a penny in for a pound, I say, so I've took out my big white handkerchief and folded it carefully over my left lapel. I was wearing a navy-blue lightweight suit, in a material called Tonik, made by Dormeuil, and I didn't want it spoiling. I don't care whether a bird uses Max Factor Mattfilm or Outdoor Girl from Woolworth's, if she starts purring up against your lapel, it won't look the better for it.

"Suppose the police were to come along," she said. They never come round there and she knows it – she's only putting that bit in to stir up excitement.

"Let 'em come," I said, "the doors is locked and the windows all steamed up. It's like an igloo in here." It was too. We were parked in this quiet little hidden away spot near the Thames at Blackfriars in this Consul de luxe 375, and Fords have never improved on that model, but they did steam up easy. "'Ere, pull this rug over you, Siddie," I said, "just to be on the safe side."

"Mind you don't ladder my stocking with your ring," she said.

"Steady up," I tell her, "I ain't no contortionist." It's not my joints I'm thinking of, it's my jacket. I don't want it messing up. I know I should have took it off, but it's too late now. You break your clutch at a time like that and you can spoil the whole thing for yourself, if you're sensitive, like I am. She starts this jockeying about. I must say she's got a handsome chest – I never knew a bird with such clavicles or whatever you call them. And talk about a cleavage! – it's like the Rotherhithe Tunnel. She's Jayne Mansfield on the surface and Mick MacManus underneath.

Now just as I'm manoeuvring a particular dodgy spot (she's got no mercy this Siddie), I suddenly hear this great loud blast in my ear.

"What's up, Alfie?" she cries out.

"Get your bloody great knee offa the steering wheel," I yell her.

"I can't!" she cries. "I can't move! I'm stuck!" That's the worst of these women with muscular legs, they go so far then they can't get back. I think they must have over-developed cartilages or something. Anyway I give her knee a good belt with my hand and knock it off, and the horn stops.

"I got the cramp in my thigh," she said. "Sorry."

"I've told you before to be careful where you're putting your leg, Siddie," I said. I open the door and get out and kind of shake and air myself. I do hate that sticky feeling you get when there's an interruption.

"I was only trying to be helpful," she said.

8

"I can help myself," I said. "'Ere, what time did your old man say he'd be waiting for you at the station at Purley?"

"Oh, never mind him."

"That's just who I am going to mind," I said. The way these birds talk about their husbands these days. "Never spoil a good thing. That's something you women can't get into your nuts. Come on now, enough's as good as a feast."

I was sorry I'd let her get me started. It's pure greed really. I think it must come from all those years you were longing for it and they wouldn't let you have any. And now you can't bear to let an opportunity go by.

Well, once Siddie sees there's nothing further going she gets out of the car and starts tidying herself up. I didn't look too closely at her because I find that dressing lark can set me off again. I mean they can say what they want about the female form divine and all that sort of caper, but if you ask me I reckon three parts of the charm of a woman is her clothes. Silk petticoats, suspenders being fastened over a nice thigh, nice black lacy bra's, and things like that interest me much more than a great big woman would, stretched out naked on a bed. I know this might sound kinky, but I believe it's dead normal.

"You soon changed your tune," she said.

"That horn put me off," I said, "– if you want to know."

I must admit I do hate a din at a time like that. She begins to pull up her stockings and straightens the back seams, and I had to admit that her legs looked real good. Then she took the white handkerchief out of my lapel.

"Don't forget your napkin," she said. I took it from her and rolled it up and started doing my toilet. I've got my own little system. First I wet it and wipe all the lipstick off my face. It's surprising how clean you can get yourself with a bit of spit and a white handkerchief.

"Know what I thought, Alfie," she said, "when I first saw you put your handkerchief over your shoulder?"

"What," I said, "– what did you think?"

"I thought you were going to take out your fiddle and play it," she said.

"Well I did – didn't I?" I said. "I come from a musical

9

family." I find with women it's not what you say, it's the way you say it. And if I get one of my comical strokes I can make most women laugh. The fact is, women don't expect you to be funny – all they want to know is, do you want them to laugh. They'll bleeding laugh. You've only to look at these Palladium comedians to know that. Then I take her bikini briefs out of my pocket and throw them to her. "Mind you don't catch cold!" I shouted.

Next I start going over my suit very carefully with this handkerchief, after I've got all the lipstick off my face. I could hear Siddie laughing away to herself and I thought: *she'll go home happy.* It struck me that I'd done her old man a real good turn, although I'd have a job making him see it. It's a funny thing, but you won't get one husband in ten feels any thanks to the wife's fancy man for the happiness he brings to the marriage.

She'd been dead glum when I met her and I'd listened to all her problems and then got her laughing. Here, now, that's a good tip for any man: if you want to *make* a married woman, the first thing to do is to get her laughing. You'd be surprised how many of them are in need of a good laugh. It don't strike the husbands. Except the ones who think they're comedians. A woman told me she once went paralysed down one side of her face forcing herself to laugh at her old man's jokes what she'd heard two million times. Yes, you make a married woman laugh and you're halfway there with her. Course it don't work with a single bird. It'll set you off on the wrong foot. You get one of them laughing and you don't get nothing else.

When I'd wiped my face and my suit down with the hanky I roll it up into a little ball and polish my shoes with it, then throw it away. That costs me two bob a time, but I find it's well worth it in the long run, the explanations it saves. And it's more hygienic.

"All right now, Siddie?" I said.

"I'm all right," she said. "What about you?"

"I'll do," I say, stretching myself out a bit and getting my jacket sitting properly. "Now what about next Thursday?"

"Same place, same time, suits me."

"Right," I say, "back into the car and I'll run you to Clapham Junction."

She puts her arm round me under my jacket and presses her finger on my backbone and runs it down inside the back of my trousers and at the same time gives me a kiss.

"Do you really love me, Alfie?" she said. That finger on the bone works if a bloke's in that mood but if he ain't in it he couldn't care no more than fly-in-the-air. I've yet to meet the woman who don't ask me that after it's all over.

"Course I do."

"Are you sure?"

"Certain to positive."

"I've got a feeling you don't – not in your heart."

"All right then, I don't. I can't win any way with you." I got the torch and shone it carefully around inside the car just to make sure everything was all right. I'm very tidy in my habits. "Now get back in the car, darling, we don't want to keep your poor husband waiting at Purley."

"He won't mind," she said, "he's used to it."

If there's one thing puts me off marriage it's married women.

"Know what, Siddie," I said as we drove off. "I think we should change our rendezvous, just in case he chances to follow you."

"Follow me!" said Siddie, "why it would never even occur to that husband of mine that any other man would want to take me out."

"That's the mistake all you married women make," I said. "You think just because your husbands was clot enough to marry you, they don't see nothing. Where d'you tell him you was going?"

"I said I was going to the pictures with Olive."

"What pictures?"

"Oh just the pictures."

"Nah, never be vague like that, Siddie. That plants suspicion."

It's no wonder there's all these broken homes, and marriages on the rocks and divorce about in these days, with women so careless. It distresses me it do. I don't know what it is about love that goes to a woman's head but it seems they lose all sense of responsibility once they start having a little affair. I offered her a Polo mint. "Here, suck one of these, Siddie," I said, "so he don't smell your breath."

"I don't care if he does smell it," she said.

I can't stand it when a woman talks like that – no consideration for other people's feelings. "Now don't be like that, Siddie," I said, "be human. You and me are having a good time, ain't we? Now why should we hurt that poor geezer. He ain't doing us no harm. Why can't you keep him happy in his ignorance?"

"All right, all right," she said.

"That's better," I said. "You go home and amuse him. Be *nice* to him – understand me?"

"Why the hell should *I* amuse him? Let him amuse himself."

"Ain't you got no heart, Siddie?"

"You want to see everybody happy, don't you?" she said.

"I don't believe in making anybody unhappy or making an enemy," I told her. You could be crossing the Sahara desert and he'd be just the geezer you'd run into, if you see what I mean. "I don't see why the husband shouldn't have a good time as well."

"So long as you don't have to give it to him," she said.

"I would," I said, "if I were built that way." And I meant it. After all, that's what we're here for in this life, to help one another. I mean so long as it ain't too inconvenient. "You don't want always to think of yourself, gal."

"What about the firm's dance?"

"What about it?"

"Well, aren't you coming? I've got you a ticket."

"Won't your old man be there?"

"Course he'll be there," she said, "but he's not to know who you are. We could have a dance together and then I could introduce you. I'd like you to meet."

Siddie, you don't know it, I thought, but you're on the way out. I'd seen it coming for some time – sooner or later they must get you to meet the old man. Once I've met the husband, it seems to put me right off the wife. I mean he could be dying on his bed but if I haven't seen him I won't think of him, will I. But once you meet and talk, like as not he'll turn out a real good sport. I don't know why but his sort usually are. Touches my heart, if you see what I mean. As I'm having it off with her I can't help thinking of him, hanging up his drip-dry shirt, or going through these garden catalogues, or taking the dog for a walk, or arguing in the pub about Chelsea or cricket or something. I don't know how it is but you seem to get a lot of his sort Chelsea supporters. They like growing roses too, if they've got a garden.

I drew to a halt beside Clapham Junction Station. "Right, gal," I said, "here you are."

"Aren't you seeing me to the platform?"

"Better take no chances, we might be seen."

"What about the dance?"

"I'll ring you at work."

"It's not always convenient at work."

"Then I'll ring you at home on Monday night – that's when he goes to visit his Mum, ain't it?"

"You can ring me any time you like at home. I don't let him answer if I'm in."

"I'll ring you on Monday when he's at his Mum's," I said. "Now goodnight."

"Goodnight, Alfie," she said.

"Now don't forget, be nice to him. And don't wear that tight skirt next week."

"No I won't," she shouted back, "I'll wear my skin-tight slacks."

I watched her running off into the station. There won't be any next week, I thought. Once a married woman gets too hot on, that's the time to cool off. They get you into trouble and it's not worth it. Her poor bloody husband, I thought. On the other hand, what the eye don't see, as they say, the heart agrees.

CHAPTER TWO

AFTER seeing Siddie off I had this other bird to meet called Gilda. I don't know how it is but I look on an evening with just one bird as only half the menu, sausage-and-mash without the treacle pud. After all, variety's the spice of life.

Matter of fact, what I like is to have three women – I don't mean all there at once, but all three on tap. And I like a bit of variety in them: one thin, one fat and one medium, or, say, one very young, one a bit older and another in between. You'll find with three like that you'll get most of your needs satisfied.

Mind you, I never like to go straight from one bird to another without a break in between. For one thing I don't think it looks nice, and for another, I find I need a bit of a change, a bit of a talk with a few mates, so I nipped into a pub where I knew one or two of my mates hang out. I don't like making fixed arrangements with anybody – I like to live in a casual come-and-go style.

I think if you were to spend *all* your time with birds you'd begin to find you're going a bit doolally. It's my opinion there isn't one in a thousand right in the head, but I must admit I love 'em. I mean they give a bloke so much pleasure in his little life. Mind you, I never fall for all that chat a bird likes to hand out about how she's given you "the best years" of her life and "you've had the best of my body" and all that sort of stuff. "What do you think I've given you?" I always say to them. I mean the man has to *give* every time, but the woman can wing it if she ain't in the mood, if you see what I mean.

There were two mates of mine in the pub, Perce and Sharpey, and they were talking to a big bloke called Lofty, a long-distance driver who actually comes from up North. Now if there's one thing gets on my wick it's when working blokes start talking about politics.

"I tell you what I think about the state of the world today," said Perce, "– I think it's dead rough."

Now what do they know about the state of the world? They only know what they're told. The truth only comes out about fifty years later.

"I think the working man has got himself all blown up with conceit," said Sharpey.

"You can't blame the working man," said Lofty, "He's brought up to believing this is the greatest country in the world – to believing we're the greatest people – "

"Aren't we?" said Perce, "I mean where's the competition?"

"I think all these wildcat strikes are making our country look a fool to others," said Sharpey. "What do you say, Alfie?"

"And you have this feeling," went on Lofty, "you'd lay down your life for your country. Leastways I had. But then as you get a bit older, you read about all them at the top – how they're all on the fiddle, dodging the income tax, entertaining, and buying their villas on the income tax –"

"The bleedin' golden handshake," said Perce.

"The working man has never been better off in his life," said Sharpey, who's never done a day's work in his life. "The engineers are asking for a thirty-five hour week and treble time for Sunday, so that if one bloke works a twelve-hour Sunday he needn't work the other six days and he's got an hour's overtime in."

"The working man begins to lose faith," went on Lofty. "He loses faith in his boss, he loses faith in the top dogs who are running the country, and he gets as he don't want to know."

"I blame the newspapers," said Perce. "I think people were happier in their ignorance. It's no use keep taking the bleedin' lid off of everything."

"You can't blame the newspapers," said Lofty. "The working man sees all these others on the fiddle and he thinks what a mug he would be to knock himself out for the country."

"Somebody's *got* to knock themselves out," said Sharpey. "You don't want the country going to the dogs. What do you say, Alfie?"

"There's only one answer to all today's trouble," I said, "and you know it as well as I do. It's human bloody nature. If you got a bloke with five kids and you scared the life out of him, like they did in the old days, that he don't get a bite for them kids or himself and his missis unless he works all the hours God sends – you'll get him working."

"My dad used to work fourteen hours a day for three quid a week," said Lofty.

"You don't notice you're working if you're dead frightened of something," said Perce.

"I wouldn't know," said Sharpey. You can say that again, I thought.

"Get the sods in debt," said Perce, "then they've got to keep working to get out of it."

"They're already doing that," said Lofty. "What do you say, Alfie?"

"If you can't scare 'em," I said, "and you can't kid 'em – you need some bleedin' big incentives to keep them working." Anyway, I thought, I wouldn't hang about here much longer, listening to that kind of chat, and as it's near closing time I decide to make a crafty getaway just in case any of them want a lift, so I drink my pint and go off and get into my car and drive off to Gilda's.

Now I've known this little Gilda for a twelve-month or more, and while she ain't exactly stupid, she is a bit on the simple side. What I mean by stupid is when a dead dim bird tries to argue you out that its stupidity is sense. Gilda don't do that. She lets you get on with what you have to say and listens. But she'd never make a number one because she's not the sort of bird you could take out and show off. In fact she's a bit backward at coming forward. She's not a good-looker, neither, not by a long chalk, although she ain't that bad, and she ain't an exciting dresser, but she's a cracking little standby. She's clean and dainty, gives herself no airs or graces, and ain't too bad on the old frying-pan stakes. All she seems to want from life is to be in love with a bloke and to think that he's a bit in love with her, if you see what I mean. And she ain't a liberty taker. Most birds go mad to get hold of a regular bloke and they've no sooner got hold of him than the first thing they think about is how to go about changing him. Now I told this Gilda from the start that I wasn't the marrying sort and she didn't mind. The trouble I've had explaining to some birds that whilst I'm willing to say I love them, I definitely don't want to marry them. Gilda ain't like that. She never tried to put the block on me, or stamp out my ego. She's always let me do what I want, have what I want and be as I am. Of course that might be another way a woman has of putting the block on a bloke. She's a very contented little gal. She's a standby and she knows it, and any bird that knows its place in this life can be quite content.

She lives in a little street off the New Kent Road, see, and just as I'm parking my car, I spot one bloke called Humphrey coming out of the house. He's about thirty-eight this geezer, but looks real old on account he takes life so serious, and he's wearing his bus inspector's uniform, which makes him look even older and more serious. I knew he must have been visiting Gilda, because we once met him together and she's told me about him, how he was keen on her before she met me.

It seems he's been married once, see, got a lovely little wife and child and his own little home and everything, when one day, the wife and kid get killed in front of his eyes, or next door to it, by a cement trailer that broke loose and crashed outside a supermarket. He's inside getting two tins of salmon for the price of one and when he comes out he's a childless widower. I hate hearing of people things like that have happened to – it makes you feel guilty because nothing like that has ever happened to you. I wiped myself over again before going in, then I let myself in with the latchkey she'd given me and crept quietly up the stairs to her room. She was waiting for me, eager and all smiles.

"I thought I saw that geezer Humphrey just going off," I said.

"Yes, he just left," she said. She always tells you the truth straight out and it's took me a long time to get used to somebody like that. I can't help feeling there's a trick in it somewhere.

"You ain't having it off with him, are you?"

"Nothing like that, Alfie," she said. "He brought me some chocolates."

"What did he want?"

"Nothing. He said he called round because he felt lonely. I asked him to stay for a cup of tea, but when I told him I was expecting you he wouldn't wait. I felt sorry for him."

"Why feel sorry for him?" I began helping myself to his

chocolates – Black Magic, just what he would buy, I thought. "What else did he tell you?"

"He told me he loved me," she said.

"The soppy nit," I said. It's the last thing you should ever tell a bird – I mean if it's true. String 'em along with it if it ain't.

"He said he gets full of loneliness and longing, seems to fill his mouth and throat and he can't taste the food he eats."

"I've a good mind to report him to London Transport," I said. "He's no right to go round on the buses in a condition like that."

She looked at me. "Do you love me, Alfie?"

"You shouldn't ask me, you know. You put me in an awkward spot. I'll always tell you if I feel like it." She looked a bit unhappy so I gave her a kiss. "Coo, you don't half pong," I said. "What is it?"

"It's Phul-nana," she said, "The scent of Araby. Don't you like it, Alfie?"

"You know I like you to smell as you are. I hate a scent covering up a smell. It's a mistake all you women make – you will not realize that a normal man prefers a smell to a scent."

"They're funny things, are men," she said. "I'll go and make some tea." She had a funny way of smiling, and you could never be sure if she was taking the mickey.

I got myself comfortable on the chair and put my feet up on the bed and suddenly felt the hot water bottle in for us. She's getting a bit previous, I thought. I knew I was always welcome, but I think it was the first time she'd put the hot water bottle in for me. Course the evenings were getting a bit chilly. A thought crossed my mind and I felt in my pocket and took out my little diary and opened it. There was a little ring round the 19th with a G on top of it. I began to feel a bit alarmed and I called out to her. "Hy Gilda, ain't today the 21st?"

She walked in out of the kitchen with some sandwiches on a tray. "Yes," she said, "why?"

"Shouldn't our little friend have arrived on the 19th?" I said.

"Our who?"

"You know, Fred," I said.

"Don't worry, Alfie," she said, "he'll turn up. He always has done."

"But he's usually so punctual," I said. He was too, was little Fred, you could almost set your watch by him. "I don't like it when he's overdue." I looked at her and to my surprise her little face looked quite cracking for a minute, nice smooth skin, with bits of roses on her cheeks and her eyes kind of nice and happy looking. "Know what, gal," I said to her, "there's times when you don't look too bad."

I always feel a bit of flattery is never wasted on a woman. I know it's the oldest thing on earth and they know it too but you'd be surprised how few men will tell a woman she looks nice. Either they don't see it or they're too miserable to say it if they do. She came over and sat on my knee. I put my arm round her and I must say she had a lovely rounded out shape to her. "How are things at the caff, gal?" I said.

"Do you know, Alfie," she said, "I took over fifty-two pounds on the till today. Isn't it wonderful?"

"What's wonderful about it?" I said. "It ain't as if it were your money."

She's got this job at a little cafe run by an Italian and his wife, where she works in the kitchen and on the till when they're serving dinners.

"No, I know it's not my money," she said, "but I like to feel they're doing well. Besides it keeps me busy, and the time passes quicker."

"Ain't it time you started that fiddle I told you about," I said, "you know, playing the piano on the till?" I just can't understand the mentality of people who are in charge of money and don't work a take for themselves. I don't mean thieving or anything like that, just the odd few bob every day. It's surprising how it mounts up. And how it makes you feel even with life.

"I couldn't do that, Alfie," she said.

"It must be the only till in London that ain't bent," I said. A bird I know is in a cinema paybox over the West and she works what they call *the pause*. Say a bloke has fifteen bob change to come – you give him his ticket and the five bob and then pause. If he's not certain or he's in a hurry he'll

19

think that's his lot, and he'll be away. She puts the ten bob note on one side in case he comes back. She reckons it's good for two or three notes a day.

"Luigi and his wife treat me like one of the family," she said.

"That's more reason to do them," I said. "You've got their confidence, see, they're not watching you."

"But I couldn't look them in the face, Alfie, if I was swindling them like that."

"Who's talking about swindling?" I said. "A fiddle – a fiddle hurts nobody. Put it all down to the larking."

"But they've been so good to me, Alfie."

"Then you don't have to do them out of nothing. You can work it all out of the customers. Tuppence here, threepence there, the odd tanner. They don't notice it when they've had a feed and they buy a packet of fags."

"But they're all ordinary people, drivers, building workers – they're just like friends. They all make jokes with me."

"But they're just the ones to do, I tell you. They trust you and they don't take much notice. How do you think these millionaires make their money? They make it out of their friends."

"But I'm happy as I am, Alfie," she said.

"You could still be happy with a few hundred pounds in the bank, instead of tuppence ha'penny. You're in a rut, girl, and you've got to lift yourself out of it."

"But I feel happier, Alfie, if I'm honest."

"You're idle, girl, that's what you are, and you think you're honest. You're mentally idle. You don't try to improve yourself. I hate talking to you like this – it makes me feel like a ponce, but somebody's got to give you a good talking-to. Suppose I'd been like that, easy going – then I wouldn't have needed no car, so's every night I'd have been running for the last bleeding bus, instead of staying on here with you."

"But I'd still be as happy with you, Alfie, if you had no car."

"Look here, gal," I said, "if you say you're happy once more I'll begin to doubt it. Straight up, I will. This world is

20

divided into two kinds of people – those who've got a car an' those who ain't. And they hate each other like poison. It's a terrible thing what you're saying, Gilda, that you're content with being as you are. It's people like you get the country upside down."

"But money isn't everything, Alfie."

You nit, I thought, you're as dim as a box of assholes. Of course money is everything – but people won't admit it openly. I mean if you've got money you can have everything – beautiful hand-tailored suits, your own car, lap up as many birds as you want, and eat and drink what you fancy – what more can any man ask for.

Course I didn't tell her all that – all I said was, "It's only people who ain't got none talk like that."

"I'm not ashamed, Alfie, I owe nothing."

"But you should be ashamed, Gilda," I said, putting an arm around her. "What you gotta get in that little head of your'n, gal, is that nobody don't 'elp you in this life – you gotta 'elp yourself!"

CHAPTER THREE

I WAS thinking as I lay there in bed in my T-shirt cotton vest beside Gilda sometime later that same night, about the first job I had when I left school, working as an errand boy in one of these sweat shops over the East End where they make boys' suits. If I don't drop off to sleep straightaway after it, I find I'm wakeful and I often go over little thoughts in my mind and memories and that sort of thing. I don't like lying there in the raw with a bird – I seem to come over clammy and sticky. Now what I used to do on that job was to knock off one of these suits when nobody was looking, nip into the lavatory with it, then I'd slip my own off, put the suit on next to my skin, and then put my own back on top. I wore a nice big jacket specially for the job. Then I'd nip home as quick as I could on one of my errands and slip off the suit. Alice, my step-mum, used to flog it in the pub of a night. She used to get as much as twenty-five bob a time for those suits, and she'd give me a dollar out of it.

Now I found that little fiddle gave me a real interest in the work, and it's my firm belief everybody should take an interest in their work. I was always willing and cheerful, and popular with everybody around the place. I could afford to be, couldn't I. Mind you, I wouldn't have been so cheerful if I'd known what I know now. It makes a guv'nor suspicious. Never be cheerful on a job if you're working a fiddle. Here, I had a nice little fiddle going a short time back, driving a lorry for one of these supermarket firms, and when we were loading up, I've got this one special loader who would always slip me in an extra crate of canned salmon and put it down to the larking. I mean I'd flog it to one of the branch managers, see, and he'd pay me half of what it was worth and I'd share the bunce with the loader. There's a special way when you're loading of slipping one in so that even when they check your load they can't count it. If done properly it's all an art.

Now one day I was loading up and whistling away when I spots the guv'nor with his eye on me. "You sound cheerful, Elkins," he says. I tumbled at once I should never have whistled. So I says, "Yeh, some mornings I feel chirpy." So he says, "You can't be feeling all that chirpy on what I'm paying you. You must be working a nice little fiddle." So I says, "That's deformation of character, mate. I'll have to see my union." And he says, "Don't come it – 'ow do you think I got where I am? I'm satisfied," he says, "so long as you do your job well and don't get too greedy, else you'll kill the goose." I was quite glad of that little tip because we had been overdoing it.

Now where was I with my little life as a boy – oh yes, knocking off these suits. This one day I gets one a bit on the large side. I go into the lavatory with it, strip down, put it on and put my other one over the top of it. I only just managed to get myself all fastened up. Now when I come up, there was the guv'nor standing there. A nice bloke he was – with a sad face that always made me feel sorry for him. "How are you liking this little job, Alfie?" he said. "It ain't bad, sir," I said, "to be quite frank, I like it. I mean, you're kept on the go, but I don't mind that. Matter of fact, I'm just dashing off this minute." Then he pats me on the shoulder and he says, "You seem to have grown a lot lately, Alfie, you're getting quite a size." "Yes, sir," I says, "that's what my mum says." "Look at your chest and your shoulders, Alfie," he says, "I can hardly believe it," and at the same time he keeps tapping and feeling around my back, shoulders and chest. "Have you anything to tell me, Alfie?" he says. "I'm in a hurry, sir," I says. "Alfie, you shouldn't have done it," he says. "Now go in there and take it off again." "Take what off?" I says. "Take this off," he says and he opens my shirt at the front, "Blimey," he says, "That's out of my top range. Now go in and take it off before I get annoyed."

Now one thing I'd learnt even at that age was that you must destroy the evidence, so I thought to myself, there's only one thing for it – down the hole it goes, and I'll flush the chain. He was standing outside and he must have read my thoughts. "Don't shove it down the hole, Alfie," he says, "you'll only block the plumbing up. The lad before you did that. Just bring the suit out as it is." I expected him to send for the police or give me a good rucking, but all he did was to take me to his office and give me my week's wages. "Sorry, Alfie," he says, "I don't think you're suitable for this job. Let me know if you want a reference." A nice bloke he was, but when I told my step-mum and my dad about what had happened, they said what a horrible thing it was for a chap to look under a lad's shirt to find his suit. Funny thing, but once you get a taste for that lark, it's surprising how it sticks with you.

CHAPTER FOUR

I'M going to call on Gilda this night and I've stopped my car at the corner of the street and I've seen this Humphrey hanging around.

"Oh, how go there," he said, "Is that you?"

"I think so," I said, "Why?"

"I was hoping I might see you," he said. He'd only been waiting for me.

"What about?"

"It's about Gilda."

"What about her?"

"Would you like to come for a drink?" he said.

"I'm in a bit of a hurry," I said. I can't bear to be with a bloke whose only to do with me is that we both know the same bird.

"I'll tell you what I wanted to ask you," he said, coming straight out with it at last, "Do you intend to marry her?"

He can't know she's up the club, I thought. "What's that got to do with you?" I said.

"Nothing," he said. "Nothing at all. I'm sorry. I know that's something between you and her. But I've always had a hope she might marry me one day."

Come to that, I thought, that might be a handy little way out of the whole business. "Why don't you ask her?" I said. "You never know your luck."

"I have," he said. "She's very kind, but she doesn't want to know. Not that I blame her."

"But you felt with me out of the way –?" I said.

"I suppose you could say that. With the coast clear you never know what would happen. And I felt if you were only passing the time –"

"Know what," I said, "I might be able to put a good word in for you."

"No thanks," he said. "I can put my own good words in – once I know I'm in the running."

"If she won't marry you now, mate," I said, "she'll never marry you." Yet I had to admit to myself there was more to him than I'd thought.

"Why," he said, "I don't know about that, I don't know at all."

"I do," I said, "so long."

As I was going off he looked at me and said, "Never is a long time." I couldn't make out quite what he meant but he had a funny way of looking. I went into Gilda's.

Somehow she looked different to me.

"Hallo, Alfie," she said. I gave her a kiss. "Would you like some coffee?" she said.

"Never shove things at me as soon as I get in, gal," I said. "I always like to get my bearings first."

"The kettle's nearly boiling."

"Never mind the kettle," I said. "Is there any news? Any reports from the front?"

"What? Oh! No, not yet."

"We'll definitely have to do something about this little lot," I said.

"I've tried everything, Alfie," she said. I looked at her. "I mean everything you hear about, Epsom's salts, gin, and some pills a girl got me."

"You mean you've been taking stuff on the quiet?" I said. "Why didn't you tell me?"

"I didn't want to worry you," she said.

"You worry me all the more," I said. "I wondered why you were looking so ropey. You don't want to make yourself ill, gal." I looked at her little face, it looked so white and pinched, I felt a little spasm of sympathy or something come over me. I put my arms round her just to comfort her a bit. She presses close up to me, must be thinking I want to make love to her but to be quite frank it's the last thing on my mind at that moment.

"You're getting very cooey lately, Gilda," I said.

She had a hurt look in her eyes and I was sorry I'd spoke. "I don't mind," I said, "except I don't like things to be sprung on me, if you see what I mean. I might not be in the mood. Love's like dancing Gilda, always take your move from the man, but be quick to follow."

"Do you love me, Alfie?" she said.

"What can I say, when you ask," I said. "You shouldn't ask you know. I'll always tell you when I feel like it." I was sorry I'd spoke to her like that so I gave her a kiss. "Here, you wouldn't fancy marrying old Humphrey would you?" I said.

"Alfie!" she said.

"Now don't get me wrong, gal," I said. "I just like to see everybody happy." The thought went through my mind

25

that they could have made each other happy. "It's regular work, you know."

"What is?"

"Inspecting on the buses," I said. "They work shifts mostly, so it wouldn't interfere too much between you and me, except nights would be out."

She took it quite calmly: "When I get married," she said, "that's one worry my husband won't have. It doesn't matter who he is."

I could see she meant it. I didn't know what to say, so I gave her a kiss. Her lips felt very full, juicy and warm. In fact her whole body felt good. "I think I will have that coffee after all," I said.

"I'll not be a minute," she said.

I sometimes give way to the quick impulse, but generally speaking it pays to pick the time not let it pick you. She went into the kitchen and I began to walk about thinking what a mess I'd got myself into. The funny thing was I could remember exactly when it had happened. It was one Sunday teatime when I hadn't felt a bit like it and somehow not having my mind on the job I'd been careless. She comes in with the coffee and a big cake on a tray. "Where'd you get that from?" I said.

"I baked it," she said. "It's an old fashioned fruit cake." You can say that again I thought. It seemed like my heart sank. I had a feeling I was being drawn into something all domestified. Funny but when I took a bite of the cake it tasted quite good.

"I've been thinking, Alfie," she said.

"Oh, yeh," I said, not listening to her. I mean what bloke wants to know what a bird has been thinking – what they say is bad enough.

"Could we go through with it?" she said.

I'd had a feeling she was going to say something like that and yet it gave me a shock when she said it.

"Go through with it!" I said, "Blimey, what an 'orrible thought!" It was too. I hate it when a woman's got something wrong with her.

"Don't worry, Alfie," she said.

"You can talk," I said. "I ain't gone through with anything in all my life. I mean I ain't in no condition for getting hitched up."

"You wouldn't need to," she said.

"I mean if I was to marry you, gal, you might gain a husband," I said, "but you'd lose a bleedin' good friend."

"I've got it all worked out, Alfie."

"You ask any *married* woman which she values most," I said. "They've all got husbands, but how many have got good friends? You can turn to a friend, but not to a husband. I don't know what you've got worked out, gal, but you gotta think twice before you turn a little creature out into this world."

"I wouldn't turn him out, Alfie."

"I don't mean *that*, turn him out – I mean bring him in."

"I'd get him adopted," she said.

"Adopted," I said, "adopted! wot are you talking about – adopted?"

"By a rich woman, see. You can read about it in the papers – how they're always on the look-out for children to adopt."

"A rich woman, yeh, I see wot you mean." I'd never thought of that. It suddenly struck me that these rich film stars were often after babies to adopt, I quite fancied the idea of a kid of mine having his own swimming pool. Not that he could ask me round but you never know.

"I'd like to do that much for him. I know he'd have a good life then," she said.

"But you can't be certain there's something there yet," I said, and I patted her little round stomach.

"In bed last night, Alfie," she said, "I thought I felt him kick."

That gave me a right shock. I mean you're standing there talking to a bird and she's trying to tell you there's a kid inside her kicking or something. "Kick!" I said – "how the 'ell can they kick? It won't be the size of my thumbnail."

"That's what they say, Alfie. I don't know if it's true. I'll tell you next time it happens and you can feel."

"You'll do nothing of the sort," I told her. "And listen if you're going to come out with that sort of chat, I'm off."

"I didn't mean to upset you, Alfie," she said. "Mrs. Artoni

used to call her husband when she was like that and it moved."

"Mrs. Artoni can call who she wants," I said, "so long as she don't call me." I'm very sensitive about such things. "D'you remember that big bird I used to dance with at the Locarno?"

"You mean the ugly one?"

"She wasn't all that ugly, and she was a beautiful dancer. I remember one Sunday night she showed me 'er operation scar what they made when she was a kid. A long scar it was with all white skin round it. Know what – I got straight out of bed, I did, an' put my clobber on. 'What's up with you?' she says, 'I'd sooner go out an' see a bleedin' horror film,' I says, 'than a thing like that.' It don't half put me off, it do."

"Alfie," she said, "can I? – can I go through with it – and have the baby?"

I looked at her and saw she was near tears and was begging of me as though I could give her the earth. Now at times like that it seems as if the mind in my head turns itself inside out and I begin to see things in a new light. After all, why should she ask me for anything. I mean, she was nearly making me feel ashamed of myself. "What are you asking me for," I said. "It's *your'n* ain't it. If you set your mind on something you go through with it. I always do. And there's nobody in the world can stop you." She came into my arms and starts sobbing fit to break her heart. "Steady on, gal," I said.

I could feel her shaking from top to toe. Now if there's one thing I hate, it's a bird getting all weepy on me. I mean, what with her face all wet and hot from tears, and the feel of those wet eyelashes on your skin, and the funny sounds they make in their throats – I mean short of giving them a swipe across the kisser and telling them to belt up you've got to feel with them. And if I once give way to my feelings I get tears come into my eyes, straight up I do, and I get a funny swallowy lump around my adam's apple. So if a bird hasn't caught you one way she's caught you another.

And there she is a-sobbing against me and I know for certain she's going to mess up the lapel of my jacket but what can you do? Anyway, I pull my jacket out and let her do it against my shirt and pat her back at the same time. Then suddenly, another thought crossed my mind. "Here, you ain't coming it on me, Gilda, are you? – trying to swing it?"

"Swing what?"

"You know," I said, "once he's born swing the old filiation order – two nicker a week until he's sixteen."

I could see by the way she looked at me the thought had never even entered her head.

"I think you know me better than that, Alfie," she said. I was sorry I'd spoke. That's my trouble. I no sooner think something than out it comes. I can't keep anything to myself.

CHAPTER FIVE

LITTLE Gilda was quite happy those months she was carrying, as they call it. (I don't know why it is but I never like coming out with words like "carrying", "expectant", "pregnant" or anything of that sort – seems like they're women's words.) At times, in fact, I thought she was a bit too cheerful. I always maintain there's a time and place for everything, and it didn't seem to be quite the right time for her having suddenly come into happiness. I mean if ever I slipped in on the quiet I'd be sure to hear her humming or singing to herself. And on Sunday mornings I'd let her bring my breakfast to bed; although to be quite frank I'd as soon get up, but you should never stop a woman from doing things for you since it only frustrates 'em. And she'd be all smiles as she popped the tray in front of me. Course it meant a little morning matinee afterwards, so in a way she was doing herself a good turn as well as me.

I like thinking things over, and the thought struck me it must bring out some new strength in a woman when she's like that. Otherwise how can you account for 'em going through months of sickness, swelling up until they're right misshaped bags, coming out in varicose veins on their legs and red stretched out marks on their stomachs, and still at the end they're hobbling about quite pleased with their little selves? Another funny thing I noticed on Gilda, she came over quite beautified, especially in the early months, both in her face and her little figure, and I told her more than once, "Blimey, gal, you ain't as ugly as I thought."

I quite enjoyed my little self during that time. Here come to think of it, these geezers in the days gone by, I mean our grandads and great grandads, whilst they might have had a lot of worries on their minds about one thing and another, I mean, poverty, diseases and whatnot, there was one trouble they didn't have – they never had to keep their eye on the calendar – know what I mean? They can say what they want about the Pill and one thing and another but one of the greatest reliefs a man can have – or a woman come to that – is to let Nature take its course. They might have had their nines and tens in families, their thirteens and fourteens or even their nineteens and twenties, with the home crowded out with loads of kids, but once they went to bed at night – or afternoon come to that – they could relax and take their pleasure as it came. You get your number one need satisfied, and I've found that after that the rest have a way of falling into place.

Mind you I didn't fancy being seen out with little Gilda after about the fifth month – not a woman in that condition or anything like that. Funny but it didn't seem to show until she was about six months gone. Little hard stomachs they've got when young, I suppose. Course she didn't mind who saw her, which only goes to prove what I've always said, that men are more sensitive than women. And towards the end I didn't even fancy being inside with her, if you follow me. It wasn't that I was nervous she'd start having it when I was around – although I was nervous that she might – it was more the feeling and I'd got myself lumbered. You get a pregnant woman beside you and you don't feel a free man any more. Right enough we weren't married, and we had no intention of marrying – leastways one of us hadn't – and she was going to have the kid adopted and in a month or two we'd be back where we started, or near enough, although you can never be dead sure after a thing like that; but I'd always been used to having Gilda around and more or less ignoring her except at certain times, but you can't ignore a woman who is eight months gone.

Well, not entirely; although I dare say you could after a few times. On top of that I used to get funny little thoughts cross my mind as I watched her padding round the room. I mean they might look a bit odd, a bit out of shape, and be troubled with the wind – at least Gilda was, and I put it down to all the fruit she ate to keep him fit – but you've got to admit it's the one time when a woman comes out superior to a man. And they do it by not wanting to be superior or anything. They can just be themselves, see. And I was able to see how some little married bloke and his wife could be quite happy over their first born.

Now if you get lots of those thoughts going through your mind they can begin to upset your way of life. I'd be out with another bird and blow me down if I wouldn't start thinking about Gilda and the kid.

Naturally I've got one or two others on the go at the same time. Same as I say, I find the ideal number is three. You can nearly always be sure at least one's in good form, if you see what I mean. If you've only two, things very often coincide. Whereas if you've got four you're apt to get rushed, to get some overlapping, and you can't concentrate on each one the same. And with three, if you've had a row with one you can keep thinking of the other two, or if with two of the other one. Always give yourself something to play with.

There was this manageress of a drycleaner's I was having it off with – I used to get my suit cleaned in the bargain. You can't turn something like that down. Her name was Milly, and I'd go round with a suit (and sometimes work a couple of ties in as well) after the shop was closed. I had my own little knock which she knew, and she'd come and let me in. She always liked to get her books and things straight first, and once she had done we'd move over to the laundry corner and have a bit of an up-and-downer amongst the sheets, tablecloths, blankets and whatnot. Now when we'd done we'd get ourselves tidy, and I'd pick up my last week's suit and we'd drive off to a quiet little pub. She always liked a Mackeson after her day's work and I'd have a pint of brown-and-mild. Then I'd listen to her troubles. You've got

31

to listen to their troubles if you want to get anywhere with a woman. They're not only in need of a laugh, same as I said, but they're longing for a chat. So I'd listen to all its little problems, then it would pay a round, then I'd pay the next round, and it's time for going. Right, I'm a Mackeson down on the deal – but I've had a suit cleaned, like as not a tie, and I've had a wrap-up amongst the sheets in the bargain. It seemed such a good bargain with Milly that it went on for months.

But in time – whilst Gilda was like that – it suddenly struck me that I wasn't really enjoying it. And by chance it came one Monday and I'd nothing I could lay my hands on to have drycleaned. So I telephones her to say I can't make it – I'd never do the dirty on a woman, have her waiting. And it struck me that night what a mug I'd been – never spotting how you can have a good time and not see that you ain't enjoying it, if you know what I mean. Course it's very hard to resist a bargain. But once I had done I began to see I'd never had Milly in the best of condition; I mean what can you expect if she'd been on her feet nine hours, her mind full of re-texing, proofing and whatnot – and come to think of it, there was always a faint pong of drycleaning stuff on her.

Now to get back to this Gilda. Once she got near her time, this Mrs. Artoni from the cafe and one or two neighbours seemed all eager to help. Funny, ain't it, you pick up the papers and read 'em and you'd think there was nothing else went on in this world but raping and coshing and robbing but once you move out amongst the people with women having kids and one thing and another you'll find people are quite kind. It surprised me, it did. They were taking over and once or twice I'd almost to remind them that after all I was the Dad.

So then in she goes to hospital. I wasn't there and I didn't see it, but from all accounts that kid comes out a treat, right bang on the minute you might say. I mean I could hardly believe it because most of the kids belonging to relations of mine were all premature or something. And never stuck their heads out of an oxygen tent until they were about six months old. They'd all two birthdays, or ages or something – the age they are and the age they would have been if only they'd have waited for the right time to be born. I didn't fancy going to the hospital to see her and I thought I'd wait until she came out, but on the Sunday afternoon I don't know what came over me but I finds myself walking round the hospital and the next thing I buys some flowers and a bunch of grapes and in I went to see her.

A funny smell hospitals have. I wonder how it is they can never get rid of it. I didn't fancy going into the ward. At first I thought I'd made a mistake and I was going out when this Mrs. Artoni came running and calling after me. I mean I'd looked round and I'd seen all the faces and I'd seen this woman sitting up in bed but somehow I'd never thought it was Gilda. Her face looked so different. Perhaps it was having had the kid, or it might have been having been looked after for ten days and having had a good rest. I can't describe it properly but her face looked very white in places and nicely rosy in others and very clean and rested.

"Hello, Alfie," she said.

"Hello," I said.

"Was you going?" she said.

"I couldn't see you," I said.

"I think I'll be going," said Mrs. Artoni. We said for her to stay but let her see we wanted her out of the way, so she went. There was a West Indian woman in the next bed and she had her husband with her and she kept waving through the window at a little girl outside.

"I've brought you some flowers," I said and I took a bunch of freesias from under my coat.

"Oh, freesias!" she said, "– how lovely. You couldn't have got anything sweeter." She gave me a kiss and she had quite a milky smell. Not unpleasant, but you wouldn't want it too strong.

"I didn't want anything too bulky," I said.

"I hope you won't mind," she whispered, "but I put my name down as Mrs. Elkins."

That's very funny, I thought, it wasn't exactly a liberty, but it wasn't like Gilda. "Why should I mind," I said, "it's a free country. Put yourself down as who you want, gal." I knew there was nothing legal to it. Just then one of the nurses came round.

"How delightful – freesias," she said. "I'll put them into a glass for you Mrs. Elkins." They created quite a stir did my flowers, and I was sorry I hadn't bought two – three more bunches.

She looked at me. "Well, what do you think of your son Mr. Elkins?"

"My son –" I said.

"He hasn't seen him yet," said Gilda.

"We'll soon put that right," said the nurse. Down at the bottom of the bed there's a little cot and this nurse dives her hands in and picks up a baby. "My, he's the image of his father," she said. "What do you think, Mr. Elkins?"

It's an odd feeling when you look down at a little ugly wrinkly redfaced baby for the first time and they tell you you're the father. At first it's hard to believe. Then you get a funny sensation, like when you're going round a street corner somewhere and you come on a military band playing.

CHAPTER SIX

THE mistake I made with Gilda was getting involved. Never get yourself involved with a bird beyond what you do together. Let her little life when you're not with her be all her own. Then you always come fresh to one another. Chat her up, of course, and listen to her – but in one ear and out the other, if you see what I mean. I was having a beautiful little life and couldn't see it. Has it ever struck you that you only see what pleasure you had in something when they take it away? I was living a full carefree life.

There was this little fat young bird from the Dials I was having it off with, Tuesdays and Fridays when her bloke was at his Keep Fit classes. He was going in for being the Southern Counties weight lifting champion or something of the sort. Whatever it was he used to ration her severely. About once a fortnight if she was lucky. She reckoned he used to whip himself up a couple of eggs in a glass of milk with a spoonful of honey in it before they went to bed, and put it on a chair, and the moment he rolled off he'd make a grab for it, and down it at once to get his strength back. She was a marvellous performer, yet somehow it never quite clicked with me, if you see what I mean. I'd always get this feeling behind my mind that she was only doing it to spite him. I suppose that's the price you've got to pay for being sensitive, feeling things like that.

I'd this chiropodist woman, Daphne, where I could slip in of a Saturday afternoon, when I'd had a few drinks, and like as not I'd get it over pretty quick – in case I went right off, because to be quite frank, she was no sex bomb as they say. Then she'd trim my toenails handsome as I was lying on the couch watching all-in wrestling. A phoney carry-on that if ever I saw one. Then on Sunday afternoons dancing at the Locarno I'd usually pull in a bird to go out with that same night. Like as not it might be a married woman. I find I go in a lot for married women, or they go in for me. A bloke like me always feels safer with a woman if she's married, and as a rule they're a lot more appreciative than a single bird. Young birds take things too much for granted. And yet with all this marvellous life going on I have to get myself involved with Gilda.

Now I called round on her in her little gaff one time, where she is with this kid Malcolm, as she insists on calling him, although I warn her he'll never forgive her when he gets old enough for giving him a handle like that. I suppose he's turned out quite a nice little infant in his way, not that I go in much for these little babies what with how they can wet you and squall and one thing and another. Mind you there are times when I look at him and people say what a marvellous kid he is – this Mrs. Artoni for instance – and I feel quite pleased with myself. Except I don't fancy it when they say Smile for Daddy and all that lark. I don't know what but it just makes me feel uncomfortable, anything like that.

Now little Gilda has taken on a mumsie look and I quite like anything like that. She's rounded out a bit see, with a nice feel of flesh to her, but not flabbified. I creep in just as she's finishing feeding him.

"Hello, Alfie," she said, "He's just going off." She gets up and puts him into his cot.

"He's got milk all round his chops," I said.

"He's ever so greedy," she said, " – like his dad."

"I expect he knows what he likes," I said.

"Isn't he growing!"

I looked down on his little face which, same as I say, had looked like a monkey's but was now turning more into a child's. "Yes," I said, "he's beginning to look quite human."

"He's gone off." She stooped down and kissed him on the forehead. Then she straightened up, fastened her blouse, picked up a few baby things and went walking towards the kitchen.

"Hey," I said, "you forgot to kiss me."

"Sorry, Alfie." She came over and gave me a peck. He's pulling her heart to him, I thought. You can't beat Nature – it has its way of looking after the helpless thing.

"Know what, gal," I said, "you smell milkified."

"Do I?" she said. "I'll go and have a wash. Make myself fresh."

"I don't mind," I said. "It smells quite mumsie." I walked up and down the room. I always do when I've something on my mind. There were lots of nappies drying and baby things hanging about. It wasn't as comfortable as it had been before. Well you get a child in the house and naturally he takes over. In fact I'd bought him a little musical rattle myself which I slipped into his cot when she was out of the way. You do something then you feel ashamed of your impulses.

She was in the kitchen and I gave a call to her: "Hy, gal, how long are you going to keep him on that breast feeding caper?"

She came in drying herself: "As long as I can, Alfie," she said, "it's the best thing for him. They make you breast-feed at the hospital, if you can, but they say most women put the baby on the bottle when they get him out, especially the young ones, they say it spoils their figures. But I promised Matron faithful I'd keep Malcolm on as long as I could."

As long as she could – how long did that mean? There was this rich woman she'd talked about. "You want to be careful," I said.

"Careful?" she said, "how do you mean careful?"

"Careful you don't get too attached to him," I said. "And that he don't get too drawn to you."

She had the sauce to laugh at me: "It's only natural we should," she said. "He's my child, and I'm his mother."

Her child – as though she made him herself! No mention of my part in the matter. "And I'm his *father*," I said. "But you've got to be fair, Gilda, you've got to think of him. What about the rich woman?"

"What rich woman?" she said, staring at me as though I'd gone mad.

"You know," I said, "the rich woman you was goin' to get him adopted to. We agreed about it all."

"I don't know about that, Alfie," she said.

"So he'd have a good chance in life," I said.

"I've got to think it over."

"You said you'd like to do that much for him."

"I can't just rush into it."

"Well you want to make up your mind – one way or another – an' pretty quick."

"Why – why should I?"

"In case he gets so drawn to you that he'll fret his little heart out when they come and take him away."

You should have seen her when I said that. "Who says they're going to take him away?" she said. She looked as if she would tear anybody to pieces that laid a hand on him. And she such a quiet little kid.

"That's what you said," I said, "– that you were going to get him adopted by a rich woman so that he'd have a fair chance in life."

"That was a long time ago, Alfie," she said, as if that was the end of the matter.

"You know what you've had, gal," I said, "you've had a change of heart. I can see it on your face. Lyin' there in the hospital must have brought it on. I could see your face changing, comin' over all soft an' mumsie it was."

She could see I'd tumbled her and she didn't deny it. "I'm not ashamed of it," she said.

"But you've got to think of him, Gilda," I said. "You could never bring him up like this rich woman could, give him the things she could give him."

37

"We'll see," she said. "I'm going back to work next week."

"She could really look after him," I said, "she could dress him handsome, give him the finest of food and the best of attention."

"She couldn't give him finer food than I'm giving him," she said, "– his own mother's milk."

I had to admit that she had me there. "And who said I couldn't dress him?" she went on. "Come here – look at him now. And look at that shawl and that cot cover. And I've got lots of lovely things for him in the drawer."

She did have him nice and I couldn't think what to say. "You can't teach him to talk nice, can you?" I said. "Not like a rich woman could." You know what you are, Alfie, I thought to myself, coming out with talk like that – you are, and a real one.

"I can if I try hard," she said.

"Not proper, you couldn't," I couldn't stop myself. Well I didn't try. "Before he can talk proper he'll be bleedin' this and bleedin' that and perhaps worse. I just heard a few kids in the street on my way in, coming out filthy they was. And who's going to look after him when you go back to the caff working?"

"I'm not going back to the caff," she said. "I'm going working on the loading bay at the brewery."

"So they've got someone else in your place," I said. "And you told me they looked on you as a daughter."

"It's a better paid job at the brewery."

"What, luggin' bleedin' beer crates about?" I said. "And you wouldn't fiddle 'em! Oh no! You wouldn't be able to look 'em in the face. Just think of the money you could have had in the bank! And tell me, who'll look after him when you're working at the brewery?"

"A woman called Mrs. Timms. She'll look after him from Monday morning till Friday tea-time. She's got four children of her own. Then I won't have to disturb him every morning, and I'll have him all the weekend."

"You won't never be able to bring 'im up like this rich woman could, Gilda."

"A child needs love, Alfie, and I can give him that."

"*Love*," I said, "*love!* A child needs a bloody sight more

38

than *love* if he wants to get on in this life." I went across to the cot and looked down at him sleeping there so peacefully. "You've got to see his side of it, Gilda," I said.

"I do, but I think this is best for him," she said.

"Well, I only wish my mum had got me adopted to a rich woman when I was a kid," I said to her. "It would've made my lot a bleedin' sight easier." And it struck me that it would too. I'd have loved if a rich woman had got hold of me – or a rich man, come to that, bent or straight, if you see what I mean. "And what about me?" I said. "You don't think I'm going to spend my weekends dodging about under wet nappies?" I don't know what it was, but suddenly the kid woke up and started crying. Gilda stooped over him and patted him.

"You won't leave us, will you Alfie?" she said.

"I'll have to think about it," I said.

"I won't never ask you for anything," she said. "Not a farthing. But don't leave us, Alfie. If you do, I'll – I'll –"

I went across to her and put my hand round her shoulder, and the kid suddenly stopped crying. "I never said I'd leave you, did I? But I felt I had to speak up because I don't think you're doing right by that child in that cot."

"I'll do right by him, Alfie," she said, "and I'll make it up to you. You'll never be sorry."

"You don't have to make anything up to me," I said, "I ain't a pimp. I'm only telling you the truth as I see it."

"Promise you won't leave us, Alfie," she said, and she grabbed hold of my jacket.

"Don't ruin my lapels, gal," I said. A woman like Gilda can't half make you feel rotten. "What do you think I am," I said, "I ain't a savage! You know I'm not going to scarper. But don't you start off crying, either, or else I'll belt you one, for sure. I don't feel up to it."

Malcolm began to cry again but I wouldn't let her go to him. "Never jump to a child at once," I said. "It don't do. You'll get more and more attached to each other and he won't even go to this Mrs. Timms." I stooped over the cot and spoke sharply to him. " 'Ere, enough of that now, mate," I said, "or else I'll give you something to cry for. Come on, now, you've had your turn."

To my surprise, he stopped crying at once and went off to sleep. What a child needs, of course, is a father's voice. I said to Gilda, "Don't forget he's got a hard life in front of him so try not to give him any wrong impressions at the start. I only wish I'd been told what life was going to be like." He opened his eyes and I could see he was going to start crying again. "Malcolm," I said, "Malcolm!" I remember how he looked up at me, and for a moment he didn't know what to do, and then he gave me a little smile or something, closed his eyes and went to sleep. I think it was just then when I first began to get attached to him.

CHAPTER SEVEN

I'VE gone over the West this Saturday morning and I've bought Malcolm a most marvellous Teddy bear. I'd spotted it in this shop window, see, and it's caught my eye and I've looked at the price, seven guineas. What a bleeding sauce, I thought, seven guineas for a child's Teddy bear! I mean there are families not got that much to live on for a week. What they'll spend on kids in these days! Mind you, I often think it's only conscience money, for how they neglect 'em, neglect to teach 'em manners and all that.

Anyway I've seen it and gone away, and then I've walked back, and I've thought I'll go in and have a look at it. Now I don't know how it is, but I can still hardly get myself to go into shops like that over the West. I mean I'm dressed as well as anybody, dressed better in fact, and come to that once you get inside it's not a very posh shop, at all. You get lots of kids milling round the place have only come to see the toys demonstrated. Anyway, I've got Malcolm on my mind – here, that's a funny thing about a child, how they seem to stick in your mind when they're very young – so I've gone in and gone up to this woman on the Teddy bear counter. Now they've got all manner of Teddies, all prices, but this is the one I want. It's not just that it's a Wendy Boston, foam

40

filled, with real nylon fur and all that, but it's the luck that the woman who made it – I expect it was a woman – has struck it off dead perfect just by chance. It's the same with most cars; you and your mate can buy two identical models at the same time from the same place, and one turns out a cracker, never no trouble, and the other turns out a load of trouble, never right.

Now it's ridiculous the very idea of paying seven guineas for a Teddy, I mean. I can go over the Lane and pick him up something that looks almost the same thing for thirty bob. But it ain't quite the same thing, that's the rub. So I find I'm dipping into my pocket, and I've took my notecase out and I'm handing over a fiver and three single pound notes, and all I get is thirteen hog change. I mean if anybody had told me a few months before that I'd give seven guineas for a child's Teddy bear I'd have told him to get stuffed. Anyway she's wrapped it up lovely and I've gone off with it under my arm and put it at one side for his birthday, a couple of weeks ahead.

Then next day comes, Sunday, and I've took him out into Battersea Park. He loves coming out with me he does. We don't take his Mum out, we just go out on our own, and all the women look at him in the park because he looks different from other kids. I know all fathers think that about their kids, the only difference in this case is it happens to be true. He's got this big mop of curly hair for one thing, and it's so lovely and silky it slips through your fingers. I mean until you've felt a child's hair you've no idea what real hair feels like. Then he's always laughing and running away. It's the same with their skin; you might think a young bird's skin is soft to the touch compared with your own, but you get a child's and it's the difference between silk and sandpaper so far as a bird is concerned. And Gilda has got him dressed beautiful, I will say that about her.

Although to be quite frank I feel she's begun to let herself go a bit to seed. Not deliberate, it's just happened that way. I'll admit it must be hard work at the brewery, so naturally she's looking a bit tired when weekend comes round, but there's no need for a body to go about moping.

I drop in every Saturday afternoon, see, and usually stay on until Sunday night, a nice little bout of family life, you could say, every weekend, which come to that is just about enough for any man. But to get back to Malcolm, same as I say, he turns out to be a smashing kid, and he's always watching out for me coming on a Saturday afternoon. That's why I never like to let him down, even when I've something better on – I mean than his mum. But one thing you've got to watch out for with a child is how it grows on you. I mean your life ain't your own once you get a kid tangled up in it. I'd only seen kids with their mums, see, for ever grizzling and griping, and you'd as soon give 'em a kick up the behind as look at 'em.

But you get a kid on his own, I mean just you and him with Mum out of the way, and it's an entirely different matter. Very soon I found I was getting quite attached to him. Now that's something I always guard against. All my life since I was a kid I've watched out against getting attached, because you get attached to somebody and sooner or later that's going to bring you some pain. And it's going to cost you some sleep. So if a bird hasn't got you one way she's got you another, for have you ever thought how though she might be as ugly as sin, something quite beautiful can come out of her?

Now same as I say on this Sunday I've had a lovely little morning out with Malcolm. And when we get back Gilda has got a beautiful dinner ready, roast beef, Yorkshire, tinned peaches and ice-cream for afters. When we've done I've put Malcolm to sleep in his cot in his little room. He won't let his Mum put him to sleep when I'm there, he always insists on me. So that gives you some idea of what he thinks of me. I've got to tell him a story or something and this time I tell him that poem about this geezer Abou Ben Adhem waking up in the middle of the night and finding an angel in his room, writing in this book of gold, and Ben asks him what's he up to, and the angel says he's writing the names of those who love the Lord, but that Ben ain't one. Anyway, Malcolm drops off to sleep in the middle of it and I tiptoes back to Gilda. She's put the dinner things into the kitchen and she's already ironing some of Malcolm's little clothes.

"What a lad he is!" I said. "He could hardly keep his eyes open but he didn't want to give in. He's going to be a real handful in a few months time. We'll have to be careful what we say in front of him. He's as sharp as a needle."

I had that feeling you get when you talk and the woman isn't listening to you. I'd sensed it during the Saturday night that she wasn't a hundred per cent with me. There's nothing like the love stakes for smelling out if a bit of quiet smouldering is going on underneath. And now I could feel it that bit more. I'd intended keeping it a dead secret about the Teddy bear but now I let it out. "Wait till he sees that Teddy bear I bought him for his birthday," I said, "You never saw anything like it. Pure nylon fur." I was going to tell her how much it cost but managed to keep it to myself. Although only just. "It's a real rich kid's Teddy," I said, giving her a hint. "I got it at a shop over the West."

That got no response, and I was looking at her from behind as she was ironing, a thought crossed my mind. "Here, gal," I said, "do you fancy an hour's kip while he's asleep?"

That's another thing I've found with a bird that when there's something not right between you it can occasionally be sorted out between the sheets, or it comes out. Mind you that wasn't the reason I asked.

I waited for her to say something but she went on ironing. "Clothears," I said, "I'm talking to you."

She went on ironing and without looking at me she said: "Humphrey's been to see me twice this week."

When she said that it gave me a bit of a shock. You know how it is – you suddenly sense something. Of course I covered up straight away. "That's very nice of him," I said, and I picked up the *News of the World*.

"He came round to the brewery at lunch time," she said.

"What's he after," I said, keeping my eye on the paper, "a bit on the side?"

"Nothing like that," she said.

"He's normal ain't he," I said.

43

"We only talked," she said.

I don't know what it was but I suddenly felt my temper rising in my throat. "Then don't effin' well tell me what you talked about," I yelled at her, "because I don't want to know."

If there's one thing I can't bear to hear about it's a bird and a bloke having their *innocent* talks together. It would never strike me to do a thing like that anyway. Here, I consider this friendly chat more intimate than the other, if you see what I mean. After all, you can work up to the other with any bird, any shape, colour or size and you needn't know a single word of each other's language to have it off quite nicely; but to sit and talk together on a park bench of a lunch-hour you've got to strike off what they call a relationship. And that can turn out to be a very intimate thing. I mean I wouldn't mind a bird of mine having it off with a bloke, say once or twice, though I'd rather she didn't let me know. I mean we can all give way to an impulse, but a relationship is quite another matter. I ain't standing for that. It goes deep – I mean with them.

"What's he after then," I said, "– if he's not after that?"

She began folding up little Malcolm's things. "He wants me to marry him," she said.

When she said that I felt a sudden cold jab near my heart. I don't know why I should, because normally a thing like that would make me feel relieved. I like that feeling of unloading the nearest and dearest birds – let alone a woman who's got herself a kid. I mean I didn't want to marry her – after all what had I to marry her for? I'd a woman supervisor with her own flat after me. But the idea there was a man wanted to marry her kind of upset me. Of course I didn't let her see it. But how to strike back, I thought.

"Does he know about little Malcolm?" I said.

"Yes," she said, "he knows everything."

Knows everything – a bleeding London Transport inspector! They couldn't tell you how to get from Jamaica Road to the Army and Navy. Come to think of it that is a bit dodgey by public transport. "And what did he say?" I said.

"He said he'd try to be a father to him."

"How can *he* be a father," I said. "I'm the child's father.

44

It's not something you can try to be."

"Yes, he knows all about that but he doesn't think it matters all that much."

"Oh, what does he think matters?"

She thought for a moment before answering: "Humphrey believes being a father lies more in giving care and attention to a child, not in just having been with his mother."

What a thing to say! He should talk! A father's a father no matter what you say.

"And in giving love," she said.

If that were true, I thought, there wouldn't be many fathers around in these days, because my married mates all they want is to get away from the kids.

"And what did you tell him?" I said.

"I didn't tell him anything."

"You must have told him something."

"I told him I'd have to talk it over with you first."

What's so funny about that? After all why shouldn't she talk it over with me? "Why talk it over with me," I said. "You're a free agent, ain't you?"

"Malcolm needs a father," she said.

What a sauce! – after I'd just bought him a seven-guinea Teddy bear! "And what do you think I am?" I said.

"I don't mean just a weekend father," she said. "The boy needs a proper father."

"We all need proper fathers," I told her, "and proper bleedin' mums, come to that. It seems there ain't enough to go round these days, so let's forget it."

"I'm not getting any younger, Alfie," she said.

"Are you trying to put the block on me?" I said.

"I'm not trying to put anything on you," she said.

"Don't talk to me any more about it," I said. "Because I couldn't care no more'n fly-in-the-air what you do."

"I don't really love him, Alfie," she said. "Not like I love you."

"Don't talk to me about love," I said. "I don't know what love is, the way you birds keep rabbiting about it. Love, love, love – if somebody hadn't told you about it you wouldn't know what the bleedin' hell it meant."

"But I do *respect* him," she said.

45

I felt dead chuffed when she said that. That's a word I'd never use, *respect*. I don't even know what it means. Well I do – but I've never respected anybody or anything in all my born days. It's not something you do or feel in my walk of life. And I expect I'll go to the grave not having been respected in turn. You can live without it. It's dying out everywhere. But what a stroke for a woman to come out with!

I got my jacket off of the back of the chair and slipped it on. She'd ruined my day. The walk to the park, the dinner, the lot, all gone sour on me. Even the old Teddy. "Then you'd better marry your Humphrey hadn't you," I said. "You've got young buster in there to think of. I'll be seein' ya – maybe." Then just as I got to the door I remembered I had her key in my pocket so I turned back and put it down on the table. "Here's your key," I said – "you might want it for Humphrey." Then I went off and quietly closed the door because I didn't want to waken Malcolm.

The thing to have done would have been to call me back. And if she'd called me back I wouldn't have gone. But she didn't and I felt a bit choked about that. It was her place to do it, but instead she must have gone on folding up little Malcolm's clothes. I couldn't get over the look she gave me as I put the key down. It was as though once having made up her mind, she was glad to see the back of me. It always gives me a shock when I break off with a woman the way it comes out that she's always harboured a grudge against me. Not just the one woman – every one of them. A man gets the idea into his head that what a bird does for him she does out of pure love – or else why do it at all? Nothing of the sort. She does it because something in her makes her do it, but if it wasn't you it would be some other geezer. And if it wasn't him it would be a cat or a little dog or maybe nothing more than a little canary in a cage. So that when you leave them they begrudge all they've ever given you or done for you. They look on it as time wasted, love lost, feelings gone for nothing. They look round for something new to love and they begrudge all that went to you. Now I never begrudge anything I've ever done for a woman. Of course, come to that, I don't do very much.

CHAPTER EIGHT

WHAT a relief it was to get rid of Gilda! I felt free
again. I don't care who the bird is or who the mate is, but
somehow I always feel better when I unload them. I mean,
if you get to know different ones intimately they begin to
stick in your mind and if there's one thing I detest it's
walking about with other people on my mind. I like to feel
free and walk about taking things as they come, thinking
mostly of myself. And it meant all my weekends were free.
That was lovely.

Course, it took me a week or two to get used to the change.
There might be lots of birds around on the loose, you can't
always get the right replacement at short notice when you
need it. I did a spell with one little bird who was kind of
romantic or something, always reading those soppy women's
picture books. Her name was Jean, but I used to call her
"Tellmesummink".

We're in bed, see, after having it off, and I've said all the
right things, or at least most of 'em, and then I'm ready for
two or three minutes kip at a time like that. I mean, I
don't go off to sleep in the ordinary sense, but I go more
into a light doze, like a bloke who's just taken some dope.
I kind of lie there on my back with my eyes closed and the
bedclothes pulled off a bit to get air to my body, and it
seems like my little imagination kind of floats away and I'm
able to hear the kids yelling in the street or somebody's
radio or telly on loud, but these things don't disturb me,
they don't even impinge, I just float away into these little
dreams of mine and I usually manage to bolster myself up
a bit – tell myself how lucky I am and, come to that, how
fortunate the little bird at my side is to have me for her
loverman, and what a marvellous time I'm having, I don't
let myself drop clean off into a deep sleep because then your
other dreams can get at you, and you can't have your own
way with them. But in this state you've got this nice light
sailing sleep and you can feed some lovely little thoughts

into your dreams – leastways, that's how I see it.

Now, I'm only in the middle of this little lot, say I've had ninety seconds of it, not much more, and I'm just drifting upwards – in fact, sometimes I'm actually flying – I mean I can fly and nobody else can and I just go wherever I have a mind – when this Tellmesummink beside me gives me a dig in the ribs with its elbow, or gets hold of me in a spot I detest being got hold of at a time like that, and it says to me: "Please tell me summink." "Tell you what?" I says. "Tell me *summink*," it says. "What – that I love you?" I says. "I've just told you I love you." I'm winging it, see, but it don't know, and I can go on for another minute or two talking like that without even waking up. "Nah, not just that," it says. "What, that you're beautiful?" I says. "Nah, not just that either," it says. "You mean that you've got lovely hair – nice eyes –" "No, nothing like that," it says. "I only want you to tell me summink." I give it up and try to drop off, hoping it might drop off or drop dead. "Please tell me summink", it says. "Two and two's four," I says, "leastways it was when I went to school." "Don't make fun, Alfie," it says, "tell me summink".

Course, I'm proper woke up by this. "What the bleeding hell do you want to know?" I says. "I don't know what I want to know," it says, "you just talk and tell me summink, then I'll know." "Do you want me to say dirty things?" I says, "Because I ain't in that mood." "Nah, nothing like that," it says, "unless they come into it." "Come into what?" I says. "Into what you're going to tell me," it says. "Go on, don't be mean, Alfie, tell me summink." "What do you want to know?" I says. I'm really getting at my wits' end now, and I'm feeling very humpty. "I don't know," it says, "I just want you to talk and tell me summink." "Well, I will tell you summink," I says, "I'll tell you this – if you don't shut your big ugly gate at once and let me get a couple of minute's kip, I'll kick you out of the bleeding bed." Do you think that stopped it? – not a bit of it. A minute later it has its little hand creeping exploring round my skin and out it comes with: "Alfie, tell me summink."

It was a lovely kid in other respects, and I didn't want to hurt its feelings, so I just said: "If I knew something worth telling, you don't think I'd tell it to a bleeding soppy nit like you. I'd keep it to myself." We'd quite a few sessions together and same as I say it was very fair in all other respects except for this habit. It would just lie there keep asking. I did throw it out at the finish. I suppose at this very minute it's got some poor geezer lying beside it and it's saying to him, "Tell me summink, please."

CHAPTER NINE

"You know what, Alfie," she said, "your heart's pumping away like mad."

"You don't expect the bloody thing to stop," I said, "at a time like this."

I was in bed with this fat little bird Clare from the Dials. Her bloke had gone to Birmingham to compete in one of the heats for the Mr. Britain competition.

"You're all lathered in sweat, Alfie," she said.

"What do you expect?" I said. I'm not a chap to boast and if I was it's not a thing to boast about but I'd definitely given her the full treatment. Mind you, you'll never get any credit from a *young* bird no matter what performance you give. They seem to think it's all a matter of acrobats; but an older bird, who's had a few disappointments, knows better. "If your bloke was in my place," I said, "and had done to you what I've just done" – I must have kept it up for nigh on two-and-a-half-hours with not more than the odd minute or two respite in between – "he'd be nothing but a blob of grease."

I knew I was right too. They can say what they want about the strain of weight-lifting, or of any other lifting, but I don't think there's any game in which a man is prepared to extend himself and knock himself out as much as he is in bed. The funny thing was the sweat really was pouring out of me. I could feel it coming out from under my armpits and running in hot and cold trickles down my body. And the old heart was thudding away like an old-fashioned donkey engine. It must have been going about a hundred and fifty to the minute. Now a bloke can often kid himself that he's having a grand passion when in fact he's simply out of condition. He hears this thudding in his ears, and he thinks the whole bleeding universe is shifting in sympathy with him, when all he needs is a good working medicine and some fresh air and exercise.

The worst of it was, I'm with this little Clare and I can't get Gilda out of my mind. Well, not Gilda but little Malcolm. I keep thinking about him, and I kind of see his Mum just behind him. Mother and child, they are one when you come to think of it. 'Course if you lose a bird you can always replace her. When you get down to it there ain't all that much difference in a load of 'em. But with children it's different – they're each one themselves, they've each got their own little nature. You'll never replace a child. You can see a school playground full of kids and not one will remind you of your own – then suddenly you'll spot a strange kid in a quiet street and you get this flash of pain in your stomach.

Now it's not only when I'm with this little fat bird but it's the same with every bird I'm with. I keep getting these thoughts about Malcolm coming into my mind. I remember our Sunday morning walks and things like that. I find I'm having birds round at my gaff staying the night even though I never have been one for all night sessions. For one thing I can never find another bird who can fall into my rhythm of sleeping. Gilda was quite good at it. She seemed hardly to breathe or stir when I was beside her. She'd turn when I turned, stretch when I stretched and sleep when I slept. I liked lying like spoons with her arms round me, her tum against my behind. And of course she never smoked, and nearly every other bird seems to smoke these days, and to be quite frank I don't like the smell of a bird's breath if it's been smoking. The things you overlook in love can come out very sharp during the night, if you see what I mean. Smells, sweat, and wrinkles and whatnot seem to come out in some birds, overnight.

And so night after night I find I'm lying there in the dark staring up at the ceiling or looking to the window and thinking about little Malcolm. Or rather I keep imagining him. And beside me some bird is snoring away without a thought in the world, and I feel like telling her to get up and get out. Except I don't like it all that much when I'm left alone.

CHAPTER TEN

"Good morning," she said, "What's the name please?"

"Mr. Elkins," I said.

"Do sit down, Mr. Elkins," she said.

I'm in this Chest Clinic place, see, and there's this woman doctor sitting at a table looking at notes. She can't be much more than thirty, but she looks older, wears specs and got her hair pulled back tight from the forehead. On first sight it struck me she might be a bit bent, but then I could see it was probably just that she'd never been between the sheets with a man. In fact, the thought crossed my mind that with regular loving and caressing – it's a must is caressing for that type of woman – she'd soften up beautiful.

"Did your own doctor tell you why we sent for you?" she said.

"Ain't it something to do with that mass X-ray that I had done down at Wimbledon which didn't come out right on the negative?" I said.

"Yes, that's it," she said, "We thought we'd have you in and check up."

"Will you be very long?" I said.

"I don't think so," she said. "Why?"

"I have an appointment at eleven-thirty," I said.

The fact was I'd got a nice little job driving a party of licensed victuallers down to Brighton for the races. I said I'd pick them up at a quarter to twelve. I didn't want to be late because there'd be plenty of dropsy if I played my cards right. Mean as can be behind a bar, they're very generous off duty. I mean I don't believe in letting my mind get soaked with thoughts about a bird I've finished with. There's a real waste of time if you like. What I always say is, get out and enjoy yourself. Enjoy yourself. She came across with a thermometer in her hand and put in into my mouth.

"Under the tongue," she said. Then she got hold of my wrist and started taking my pulse or something. She looked at her watch then looked very closely at me.

What got me was the way she said it, *I don't love him but I do respect him.* Same as I say, I don't want any bird's respect. I wouldn't know what to do with it. I mean it's time enough for that when they've nothing else to give, if you see what I mean. After all, she's told me time and time again she loves me, loves me for myself, whatever that might mean. But I ain't ever told her I love her except at those times when you've got to say something just for appearance's sake.

She took the thermometer out of my mouth, wiped it very carefully with a piece of cotton wool, had a look at it, then put it into a jar of some stuff on the table and flung the cotton wool into a basket under the table. Here, that's a funny thing about love, the way it has of going off, like yesterday's milk, I mean, if it's not kept at the right temperature.

"How did you get here?" she said.

"I walked here," I said.

"Did you feel tired after it?" she said.

"Tired!" I said, "It's only ten minutes' walk. No, I didn't feel tired." Then I said: "I'd have come in my car only there's no proper parking."

"Have you lost any weight recently?" she said.

"My weight never varies," I said, "I'm always the same, eleven-six. It's the weight I've been for years."

"Would you take off your jacket and step on the scales, please," she said.

I took it off and put it on the back of the chair and then I stood on these scales, and she began moving the sliding things about. I mean I've always stuck to my side of the bargain with Gilda, but a bird will never stick to its side. A bird will only do what its feelings tell it to do. It won't take any account of what's been said and done. And once a bird turns you've had it, you're out in the bleeding cold.

"Ten stone nine pounds," she said.

"Get off!" I said. "Are you sure these scales is right? I can't believe it!" I felt at my waistband. My trousers did feel on the loose side. "Course, you've got to take into account this suit, I mean these trousers don't weigh nothing. It's a ten-ounce mohair and worsted."

"Would you take your shirt off please," she said.

Now there's one thing I never do with a woman, I never crawl to one. They've got to take me as I am or not at all, if you see what I mean. I took my tie off, well just loosened it, see, and pulled it over my head. I mean if you keep knotting and unknotting a tie you'll get creases all over the place. The best thing is to get a good knot and stick to it, just loosen it, see, and pull it over your head and hang it up on the back of a chair or something. Then I took my shirt off.

"You look brown, Mr. Elkins," she said, looking me up and down.

"Yes," I said, "I've had one or two afternoon over at the Oasis at the top of Shaftesbury Avenue there. It's quite a good eighteen pennyworth once you get inside." It was, too, you get 'em all shapes and sizes.

"I shouldn't do too much sunbathing if I were you," she said.

What a thing to tell you in this country, I thought, and what a load of red tape! They only want to do you out of your share of the sunshine, what bit there is. I could see her staring at my chest and that. Now, I'm not a muscle man, not even got a big chest or anything like that, I've got more of a bony frame which don't seem to have changed much since I was a lad. Now it's funny but women seem to go for that sort of thing. They don't go for these great big hunks of beefcake as they call it, they like a bloke like me that they can take into their arms. Leastways that's the way it's always struck me. They like the contrast – hard and soft.

"Do you perspire," she said. "I mean, do you sweat much?"

"Sweat," I said. "No, I'm not really a sweaty type. Come to think of it, I did sweat a lot last Sunday afternoon at the Locarno, but I was dancing and I'd had a few beers, so I suppose anybody would sweat under those conditions."

There's a real dream I used to know called Kenny, bent as can be, used to hang about transport cafes, absolutely gone on drivers he was, went in for trunkers mostly, long-distance men, see, wouldn't touch the blokes on local runs, and one time he saw me with my shirt off – but my trousers on – I'd been having half an hour's kip in the sunshine, lying on top of my load, and this Kenny looked at me and said, "Alfie, that body of yours would pull any bint. It's so appealing, so lean but so substantial. It's making me go funny at the knees." So there you are, if you can take the word of a brown hatter – and I don't see why not.

She kept looking at me with those big brown eyes of hers, so innocent like, that I found myself keeping on talking. "I'd say I sweat like any other bloke in the normal way. Of course I use a deodorant under my armpits. You just rub it on, quite good they are."

"And do you ever sweat at nights?" she said.

"I should think nearly everybody sweats at night one way or another," I said. "Do you mean in bed?"

"Yes, in bed," she said.

I remembered getting all lathered up that night with young Clare, but I didn't mention that because I didn't feel it came into it.

"Some nights you go to bed cool," I said, "and if the weather comes over hot in the night you naturally start to sweat a bit. Of late I do find myself throwing off the eider-down." In fact it's an old topcoat, officer's, but she's not to know that, is she?

She got me down on this chair and put this stethoscope thing on her ears and began tapping my back and chest.

"Take a deep breath," she said. "Now breathe out slowly."

Did I tell you about this letter I got from her, saying that she's only decided to marry this geezer Humphrey?

"Say ninety-nine."

"Ninety-nine."

Me and Malcolm will be all right because then I shall be able to stay at home and look after him, she writes.

"Again –"

"Ninety-nine."

But what about you Alfie, what will you do? Won't you miss us? Know what! – I came over dead choked when I read that bit in her round writing. Fancy her thinking of me like that! Of course, I managed before I ever met Gilda and I'll manage after she's gone.

"Do you ever feel any pain in your back?" this doctor said.

"Pain," I said, "pain?" There are times when you've got a pain and you don't know you've got it till it stops, if you see what I mean. Pain's a funny thing. You can have a pain in your heart and it can make you dead sick, but you can have a pain in your back and not know it's there. "No, I've got no pain," I said. She went on tapping away at my back. She had quite nice hands, on the stubby side, but they're sensitive. "Funny," I said, "but I believe I've a pain there now. Seems like I just felt it this minute."

"Where?" she said, "– there?" She sounded quite pleased.

"A bit over to the left," I said, "a bit higher up." She tapped me a couple more times and I let out a wince. "There!" I said. "Yes, there," I said.

"Is it tender?" she said.

"It is when you prod and mess it about," I said. "It ain't too bad when it's left alone."

She came round front and started sounding my chest. "Do you cough much?" she said.

"I cough of a morning," I said, "but then everybody does after that first cigarette." I find I'm missing her, so after that letter I stick it out until the weekend afterwards comes round and then I go and visit her.

"Do you bring anything up when you cough?"

"Up? No, not much, just clear my chest, see. Well that's the point of coughing ain't it, to bring something up and give the tubes a good clearing out."

"Breathe in deeply again," she said, "and hold it this time." I took a deep breath and held it. Know what? She doesn't want to let me in. I had to knock, of course, because I'd given her my key back. She kept me at the door but little Malcolm was inside and he heard.

"Let it out slowly," she said. I was nearly bursting so I just blew it out. She was in front of me and it went into her face, so she just put her finger up and put it against my nose and pressed my head to one side.

"What's up?" I said.

"Will you please keep your head turned away from me," she said, "as you're breathing out."

You think you know a woman, but you don't. A man can never know any woman. "Keep your head turned away from me as you're breathing out!" Not a nice stroke to come out with at a chest clinic. Anyway, same as I say, little Malcolm heard me so he came running to the door. He's not going to see his own Dad turned away, so she had to let me in. Know what, she wouldn't let me touch her. She drew back she did. After all those nights we'd had together.

"Breathe in again, Mr. Elkins. A good one this time."

They're all bleeding good ones, I thought. I took a deep breath.

"Breathe out slowly," she said.

I gave a sharp turn of my head right away this time, and blew my breath towards the far wall. I can let a woman see when she's hurt my feelings. Now that's a thing I've never done – refused a bird. Not if I was on my death-bed.

"Say ninety-nine."

"Ninety-nine."

"Ninety-nine."

"One hundred."

"What?"

"Eh? Oh, sorry – I wasn't thinking. Ninety-nine."

"Breathe in once more. Good. Now breathe out slowly."

I've had my share of ugly birds. Some of 'em getting on in years – some right old boilers you might say, but I never said no, if you see what I mean. And it hasn't always been easy. Yes, I've got my code of honour and I've always stuck by it – but a bird don't know the meaning of the word. Sorry, Alfie, she says, but I'm going to play fair by Humphrey, the same as I always played fair by you. Played fair by me! Why, she never wanted any other bloke when she had me so what playing fair was there in that? She was making a virtue out of her own natural inclinations. And her and this nit Humphrey have got together and gone and taken my little son away from me.

"How do you feel, Mr. Elkins?"

"Never felt better in all my life." So I put young Malcolm down and I go off. I've got my pride, ain't I? "I mean, I felt good when I was walking here in the sunshine this morning – my mind was on Brighton races – I've got to drive a party down before lunch, see, but come to think of it, I do feel a bit duff this minute." Of course young Malcolm begins yelling "Daddy!" after me. He wouldn't stop yelling "Daddy".

"Have you been worrying about anything lately?"

"Who, me? worry? I ain't the worrying sort. You must be able to see that." Fancy asking me a question like that. I'm wearing this lovely suit, she's seen the Swiss nylon shirt, and I've told her I've got a car, so why should I worry. Know what, there are times when I imagine I can still hear him calling "Daddy" after me. I think it must be your thoughts that make sounds in your ears. "Well, we've all got some worry or other, ain't we?" I said, "I mean, you're not alive if you ain't worried about something or other." There's a difference between worrying and being a worrier.

"Mr. Elkins, do you find that you get quickly irritable of late?" she said, as though it was of interest to her.

"It's very funny you should ask me that," I said, "but I do seem to do my nut very easily these days."

"You what?"

"Blow my top. I get all aeriated over something or nothing. Yes, get irritable."

"Do you sleep well?" She was jotting it all down. I sometimes think these doctors can't see the complaint for the notes.

"I no sooner put my head on the pillow than I'm off."

"And what time do you wake up? Oh do put your shirt on."

Apart from that one little nasty remark earlier on she was quite a sympathetic woman. I thought: I suppose you've got your own problems like the rest of us. She could be in love with a specialist who don't want to know. I began to put my shirt and tie on.

She went on making these notes and watching me at the same time. "I used always waken up when it was time to

57

get up," I said. "If I'd a little job starting early I'd waken up early, and if I'd a job starting late, I'd waken up late. I never needed no alarm clock."

"And what about now?"

"I always wake up dead on the same time – four o'clock in the morning. And that's no matter how much I've had to drink and –"

"Do sit down Mr. Elkins. Yes?"

"Thank you. Can I be frank?"

"By all means," she said. "You can tell me everything." I felt like saying: "I love you, darling. All my life I've been searching for you and now I've found you." In fact I nearly did say it. After all, there's not many birds you can tell *everything* to. Behind her specs she had quite nice mumsie eyes. I felt I could unload some of my troubles on her. After all, she was getting paid for it. "And no matter who's beside me, if you see what I mean."

"Yes, I quite understand," she said. You think you do but you don't.

"I find I'm lying there in the dark, staring up at the ceiling. Or looking for light coming through the window. I keep thinking about this child I used to know. "A child?" "His name was Malcolm. I was friendly with his mother. Nothing very special, she wasn't. She was just an ordinary gal, but I knew him well, the child, see." What am I going on about, I thought. She got up from the table and walked across to a frame. There was a big X-ray or something hanging on it.

"There is something I must tell you, Mr. Elkins," she said. I was just thinking how young Malcolm had come out of my loins, as they say. Well anybody who comes out of your loins is bound to be part of you. She switched on a light and this X-ray lit up and showed up a load of dark ribs.

"I'm afraid there are two shadows on your lungs," she said.

"Shadows on my lungs!" I said. "Shadows on my lungs! What kind of shadows?" Did that mean a lot of rotten microbes were chewing away at my lungs this second. I was wasting away. For a minute I felt scared out of my life. I felt the sweat pouring out in cold trickles from under my armpits. Then all my back seemed to turn into a mass of pains. There seemed to be a black shadow coming down over my eyes. Then I began to feel paralysed. She went on talking about rest, but I seemed to have gone deaf. My feet went heavy as lead. It was like they'd tied weights to them. I tried to stand up – I don't know why. I could hardly rise. Oh Christ in heaven help me, I said inside myself. Then I felt the room getting a bit dodgey about me. And I fell very slowly down on my face, and I remember I was thinking: *Oh Christ in heaven help me.*

BOOK TWO

"What use is money without good health?"

CHAPTER ELEVEN

ONCE you know you ain't going to die it's funny how soon you pull back to normal. Mind you, I'll never forget that first night in the sanatorium – my pillow was all wet with tears. I turned my face into it, so's nobody would hear me, and I sobbed my little heart out. What I thought about mostly was how I was lost amongst strangers and at the same time there was all these birds that loved me, who I'd only to raise a finger to and they would do anything for me. But we were separated and they could do nothing for me. And I didn't really like any of the nurses at first, except this one, and she was a bit crippled, leastways she had a funny hip or leg or something. She was really a staff nurse, and she was the only one who gave me a special look. When I say special I don't mean anything very special, but that look a woman gives you with her eyes that she ain't handing out to every Tom, Dick and Harry. I was very thankful for that little look. I felt like saying to her: "Why don't you and me go off an' live together in a little cottage somewhere and you just nurse me and nobody else?"

The fact is, when you've got this T.B., you might be weak, but you've got this temperature, and when you see these fine strapping nurses stooping over beds and that, you can hardly stop yourself from getting out and going at them. You find yourself thinking of nukky night and day – and it's all around you, but you can't have any. Now I always say it's something you should *never* think about – you should have it. Thinking of it is unhealthy. In fact, it's unclean, if you see what I mean. Although that might be coming it a bit too strong.

When I'm in a position like that, I mean amongst a lot

of other men in a bunch, it seems my soul shrivels right up into a tiny little nut or something and it's as though I'm a child longing for its mum again. I'm definitely the sort of bloke that needs a woman around, because a bunch of men are just a lot of berks so far as I'm concerned. Then about midnight on this first night I must've started dozing off when I hears this bloke in the next bed to me yell out: "Who's that? – Who's there? – Who is it?" And a woman said: "It's me – Nurse!" "Oh sorry, Nurse," he said, "I thought it was my wife Lily – she has a way of walking about the home doing jobs when I'm half asleep. I must have been dreaming about her. Goodnight." One time I'd have thought, you poor soppy bastard, why don't you catch up with yourself? But I didn't on this night, I thought instead: I know how you feel, my old son.

The next thing it started raining heavy and I could hear all these dripping sounds of the raindrops hitting the leaves on trees and dropping off dripping onto the ground. It sounded so lonely it did.

CHAPTER TWELVE

Now when morning came round and the Night Nurses started washing one or two of the patients and handing out wash bowls to others and the tea came round and everything got going with the Day Nurses coming on duty and the sun shone through the windows, life began to look a bit different for me. There were one or two blokes that thought themselves comics and they started pulling the nurses' legs, and everybody is calling out Jack, Joe, Len and Alfie as though you'd known each other all your lives, I found that I was joining in and after a day or two I was one of the gang.

It was an eye-opener to me, mixing with the different sorts in there, and chatting them up. I will say this for hospitals, they make for sociability. There were these two blokes, civil servants, one in the Ministry of Pensions and the other worked in Whitehall, not topdogs, mind you, clerks of some kind, earning about nine hundred a year or a thousand topweight, and how they ever got T.B. I do not know, but it certainly couldn't have been the work: they were underfed I reckon. Course they were both buying their own houses, one at Bexley Heath and the other near Dulwich, and after paying thirty years or more they'd actually own them. You know the sort of bloke I mean, leaves home every morning with his dark suit and umbrella, *Daily Telegraph*, and a strict ration of half a dozen fags in a packet, one to smoke on the train, another after morning coffee, one and a half over lunch and so on. God help them if a mate – I mean a colleague – borrows one. They might occasionally celebrate of a Friday, say if England wins the ashes, and they'll be so carried away they'll go into a pub for a drink. Sure enough they'll both have a touch of the shoe-lace – stoop down fastening their shoes when it's time to pay. Mind you, they love their own little lives.

They were nearly always talking about money, in one form or another, about the best buys in *Which* and so on. At one time I heard them talking about insurance. One was saying what a contented mind it gave him to know the wife and kids would be well looked after if he snuffed it. Then the other says what a marvellous bargain he'd struck with one insurance company – so far as he could make out he couldn't lose, and if he were to die within the next five years he'd show a big profit – not that he did *want* to die, but it was as well to know that if he did he'd got the better of the insurance company. So from insurance they went on to death, and one said he'd left strict orders to be cremated, it being very thoughtless in these times for blokes to get buried, what with all the shortage of land. He went on to say how comforting it was to think that the nation would be able to grow a few extra cabbages in the space his grave would have taken up. I never saw blokes worrying so much about how the world would carry on after they'd gone. The other said he agreed, but as there was room for one in his mum and dad's grave he felt it would be a pity if it went to waste.

Same as I say, though when you know you're not going

to die you quickly grab the oars and pull yourself back to normal. I'd been thinking of God and death and how if what the teachers at school told me, and the Bible were true, I'd definitely be in for it. It seemed I had very little to show for my life on earth. But who has? I remember once going on one of the cheap holiday fortnights to Majorca (what don't turn out as cheap as you think), and on the 'plane we're all knocking back this tax-free whisky, when the thought struck me: *Suppose we should crash?* That would mean you'd go in front of the Judgement Seat (that's allowing there is one) and you'd be pissed to the wide, and the Archangel or somebody would say, You've been thirty years down there and you come before your God as drunk as assholes. What a liberty to take! Know what – I never touched another drop the entire flight!

Mind you, I wasn't sorry for the things I'd done so much as now it seemed a waste of time to have done them. I reckoned that if I had my lot to come over again I'd have tried to live different. Not, when I came to look at it, that there would have been much chance. You can only be what you are, leastways that's what you tell yourself. I didn't have these *thoughts* all the time, but they had a way of sneaking up on me between seven and nine of an evening before Nurse gave me my sleeping tablet.

But once I felt the old blood hurrying along through my veins again, and woke up of a morning feeling nice and chipper, all them things blew clean out of my mind. Course it doesn't half change your way of thinking being in a place like this – next to death's door. I could honestly recommend for anybody to get a bit close to death, it makes you see life better. Not too close, it ain't comfortable.

I used to think money was everything. I really did. I've *said* money was everything. If you've got money, I used to think, you can have everything, handsome suits, your own car, lovely nosh-ups and beautiful birds – now what more does any man in his right mind want. But now it turns out it's not so. All those things are not a bit of use without your good health. What's the use of ten thousand nicker in the bank and you've got a great horrible pain in the guts? I've come to see that your health is of primary importance.

Here, I've looked through this window here in the sana-torium and I've watched one bloke sweeping up the leaves along the path. Now in civil life I wouldn't have looked twice at a bloke like that. In fact my eyes wouldn't have seen him. I'd have struck him off the list of things to see, I'd have put him as being beneath consideration. He's earning twelve quid a week, say, or at a pinch we'll put it up to fifteen for him with overtime; and he's out in all weathers, day in, day out, year in, year out, just sweeping up leaves. Just think of it! Never a change – always, or nearly always the old broom handle in his hand. On top of which he's probably got a great hulking fat wife at home who spends all day rabbiting with the neighbours and dashes in ten minutes before he's due home and starts rushing about making out she's been at it all day. Like as not she's had half her inside taken out on the National Health, her sort usually have, just to attract attention. Whenever she does cook she makes him these horrible home-made dinners of stinking stuffed heart or something what you can still taste a fortnight after you've had it. He's got three or four real ugly kids, perhaps more, since he couldn't be more miserable if he had a dozen, and they've never done wanting. Into the bargain he's paying for one to learn the piano, another to pass exams, and no doubt he's got a real fat-ankled, toffee-nosed daughter who wants to be a ballet dancer. And of course, from Mum down they all despise poor old Dad for being a streetsweeper. I don't have to go on – you must know the sort of family I mean. Now I've watched that man through the window for many an hour on end, sweeping up leaves, coaxing the odd diffi-cult turd on to his shovel and in my heart I've envied him. I've envied him being out in the fresh air for one thing, whilst I was in bed. I've envied the energy he had to push that big sweeping brush about when I've hardly the energy to sit up. And I've envied him his health. And I've even envied him getting into bed every night with this great slut of a wife and having it off. Oh the things I could tell about myself if I were to let myself go!

I've thought, Alfie, it doesn't matter what problems you've got or how simple your little life is, if you've got your good health you're not too badly off.

Here, there's this chap in the next bed to me, a bloke of thirty-five, called Harry Clamacraft, comes from Slough, he's married with three kids. His wife comes every Sunday and brings him her own marmalade. Shocking stuff, chew, chew, chew – digestive biscuits what give you indigestion, and a load of such rubbish. But she's a nice, kind woman, see, and they're gone on one another. Harry – Lily: Lily – Harry, they're each other's world, together with the kids.

I remember one particular Sunday, he's sitting up there in bed waiting for Lily to visit him. He's had nothing else on his mind since the Sunday before, and I'm watching him as he pretends he's reading, and yet I know he's got his ear cocked listening for her footsteps, because you get as you can tell everyone. I also know that it's an odds-on bet she'll be late. After all, she's got these three kids to attend to before she leaves home.

Now this Harry is a real decent bloke – though not the sort of chap I'd care to mix with. He's a motor mechanic, see, and for months on end he's been working overtime every night till about ten o'clock. This is so they can buy their own home and pay for all the furniture they've bought on the knocker, and of course he's making his guv'nor a fortune in the bargain – the way these garages overcharge these days – and he's paying his bit of income tax to help the country keep going. You can bet that about three-quarters of Harry's money is spoken for before he even begins to think about himself. Now the next thing, poor Harry goes down with T.B., which puts an end to all his striving. What's the answer? – I don't think I'll ever know.

Anyway, being in the bed next to him I've been watching him and studying him and I can see that he's been worrying that much about his wife, and his family, and their little home, and the payments on it, and even about his guv'nor, and his job, that I get to wondering whether Harry is ever going to go out of that place alive. I mean they've got T.B. pretty well tied up these days, what with all the new drugs and that, but if you get one chap worrying it seems nothing in this world will get him right.

66

I know there's no visitors coming to see me, so I can relax. I've written and told everyone that I know that I'm on silence. Not allowed to speak, see. What a stroke, eh? Well, to be quite frank I didn't write that straight off; in fact I'll admit I was longing to have some mate or some bird call and see me when I was first in. So I wrote a few letters off and I got replies from some saying that they were coming as soon as they had a clear Sunday. Course the clear Sunday never came round. So I wrote back and told them not to come, that I wasn't allowed to speak. I've got my pride.

I decided this was a very good little tactic of mine because I'd be propped up there in my bed just watching how nervous and eager the others were waiting for their wives and friends to come. In that way they all let themselves get dependent on these others coming, and I believe it doesn't do to be dependent on anybody in this life. Once you get dependent you're a free man no more. And after all, who wants visitors? They bring their flowers and fruit and whatnot, and they tell you how well you're looking, and they've only been with you for about five minutes when their eyes begin to shift about from one spot to another, up and down the ward, and you can see they're dying for that bell to go so's they can get away. I've watched them closely. Then they've no sooner got out of the door than they say to each other: "Coo, did you see poor old Ned? Don't he look rough! I didn't like the look in his eyes. Did you see the way he kept fingering the sheets. Keep them insurance policies dusted. Don't throw that black hat away." This is not kid, I've actually heard them. You can't blame them, because after all they're only human.

Now on this afternoon I have in mind I'm already up and about in my dressing-gown, and Harry's sitting propped up in bed pretending to be reading, and of course the bell's gone and they all come flocking in, except Lily, Harry's wife, when I spots one chap called Joe Holland, a retired cab-driver.

"Howgo, Joe," I said, "How're things?"

"Rotten," said Joe.

"Is the old stomach playing you up, Joe?"

"We're playing one another up," said Joe.

They're nearly all the same these old taxi-drivers, they've all got bad stomachs. "Are you just off visiting old Hardbattle?" I said.

"Yeh, I've brought him these apples," he said.

"But he ain't got no teeth, Joe," I said.

"That's why I've brought 'em," said Joe. "He never was any bleedin' good."

"What do you come for, Joe," I said, "if you don't like him?"

"I feel happier with people I don't like," said Joe. "Then it gets me out of the house on a Sunday, which is quite a job in these days. And of course it does me a world of good to see that basket lying there on his back and me still on my two feet. The worse he is the better I feel when I leave him."

Now I've just been talking about money and here's a very good example in this Joe Holland of how once you get hold of money it gets hold of you. He once told me when he was young he scrimped and saved every penny, he worked all the hours God sent and he never had time for a decent meal.

Old Joe tucked the apples under his arm and rubbed the palms of his hands across his stomach and let out a little groan.

"Why don't you see a Doc about your stomach, Joe?"

"I've seen dozens. I've even paid. I've been to Harley Street. They can't do you a blind bit of good once the stomach lining's gone. I'll bet I've got a score or more bottles of medicine on the kitchen shelf. I never know which one to take. You can bet this, if a medicine's going to ease you now it'll cause you pain later."

"What they call the side-effects," I said. "How did you get it, Joe?"

"Keeping the wheels turning. I never had time to stop for a decent meal. I never went on a holiday or nothing."

"How was that, Joe?" I've heard it all before, but it costs nothing and it gets the visiting period over.

"Saving up, see. I'd got it into my head I'd retire early, and I told the missus we'd get a little bungalow down by the sea at Peacehaven once the kids were off our hands. I was very ambitious, see. She was always wanting to go on holiday but I kept saying as how it would hold us back. I didn't like breaking into it, see, I mean my capital. The more you have the more you want. Money's a drug, and the ambition kept me going."

"Mind if I have one of your apples, Joe?" I said.

"Help yourself," said Joe. "You'll find them on the sour side."

I took a bite of the apple.

"I envy you your teeth," said Joe.

"Won't old Hardbattle be waiting for you?" I said.

"Nah, he's just about as glad to see me as I am to see him."

"You were telling me you were saving all this money up, Joe. What happened?"

"Well, I've got a few hundred in the Post Office Savings, see, and some in building societies, and I decide to buy some brewery shares seeing as how everybody I know seems to spend half his money on beer, and of course I've got some money hidden away in places where the Income Tax bloke can't get his hands on it. I mean for a taxi-driver I'm quite nicely fixed."

He stopped. "Go on, Joe," I said, "what happened?"

"Well, one Sunday dinner time my poor missus goes and kicks the bucket. Just like that. Heart, see."

"Get off, Joe!" I said. He words it a bit different every time, but in the main it's the same story.

"Yeh, the dinner all ready to serve, the joint out of the oven, the gravy made, and she just slumps off on the kitchen floor like that. I can't remember what she last said to me. It was as though she'd gone off and left me without a word. And yet in all the years she never once missed waving me off through the window."

"Did you miss her, Joe?"

"Oh, terrible! – especially after the funeral. That's when you feel it," said Joe. "We weren't all that *fond* of each other but we were very *close*, if you see what I mean."

"I think so," I said. "Carry on."

"I'd just turned sixty-five, ready to retire," he went on, "and I found the day traffic getting a bit dodgey, and what

69

with all the one-way streets and the traffic blocks, I decide to go on nights. As a matter of fact, I hadn't been sleeping the same without my missus."

"Get off, Joe," I said. "You mean – ?"

"I don't mean what you mean," he said, "all that came to an end long ago, except for the very occasional Sunday afternoon."

"How does it feel when that stops, Joe?" I said. "It must be awful."

"It's a relief, mate, a relief," said Joe. "You'll find when you get my age you go in more for relief than for pleasure."

"How do you mean, Joe?" I said. It was a new tack.

"Once you turn sixty," said Joe, "pain starts gettin' at you from every end. All you look for from life is a bit of relief. Nothing else."

"You mean you ain't interested in crumpet any more, Joe!" I said.

"It hardly ever crosses my mind," said Joe. "The only time it does is when you begin to wonder why you ever knocked yourself out so much all over a miserable two-three minutes of skin rubbing with one another. I'll admit there's the odd little memory of a particularly good one, but you'd be surprised out of all the tens of thousands of times you've done it how few times come back to mind."

"How come you couldn't get sleep then without the missus?" I said. They can be very depressing some of these old geezers, the things they come out with.

"She used to put her legs over mine in bed, she'd varicose veins, see," said Joe. "It was uncomfortable at first but somehow I got used to it. I don't half miss them legs. Anyway I find driving at nights ain't no pleasure, what with all the lights and my eyes getting a bit dicey, and all these young villains about these days, so I packs the whole thing in. I'm what you call financially independent."

"You're on a soft number, Joe," I said.

Joe shook his head. "I ain't. It's bloody awful. You don't know how to fill your time in."

"Don't you like a drink, Joe?"

"The old stomach won't stand it. I come over in acidity. It's all the fumes I swallowed and the meals I missed."

"Here, didn't I understand the last time I saw you, you were going off on one of these eight-day coach trips to Paris?" I said.

"I came back on the second day by train," he said. "The food was upsetting my stomach. Then I couldn't get my missus out of my mind. I kept thinking how she was always longing to go on a little holiday and somehow I never took her on one. It was like she was looking over my shoulder all the time."

Remorse, see. So if a woman hasn't got you when she's alive she's got you when she's dead. Lily, Harry's little wife, arrived just then, all hot and bothered. Joe turned away from me to watch them. He seemed to like the little scene.

"Oh, I'm ever so sorry I'm late, Harry!" said Lily. "I couldn't help it!"

"It's all right," said Harry.

"I started from home early enough. Then everything went wrong at the station. You look worried."

"I was only worried for fear something might have happened to you," said Harry. "I'm all right now you've come."

I waved across to Lily and she smiled back. She'd quite a sweet little face when she smiled. Course they're only interested in their husbands, women like that. It's a kind of 'poor-you' smile they give, what a pity you ain't got a nice little wife like me to look after you. She went on telling Harry about how she couldn't make up her mind whether she should take a taxi or not after she'd helped an old lady off the train with her luggage. Then she began to empty her basket and although old Joe was supposed to be talking to me he kept watching them.

"There's your new laid eggs," she said, "and there's your digestive biscuits, and there's your home-made marmalade." Those bloody great chunks of peel in it. No wonder poor Harry don't get well.

"What did Doctor say," she said. "Is he satisfied with you?"

"He says I'm not doing too badly," said Harry. "I might soon be an up case." More like a bloody nut case,

I thought to myself, the way you're going on. I mean he'd been waiting there a half an hour for her and never said a word when she arrived. I'd have given her a good rucking I would. Helping some old lady off with her luggage and she misses the bus whilst her poor husband with his face all washed has his eyes skinned for a sight of her. It's keeping things to yourself makes people ill in my opinion. Out with it.

"Did that bloke come about that smell down at the bottom of the garden?" said Harry. The great romantic, I thought. His wife comes to visit him once a week and all he can think of is the smell down at the bottom of the garden.

"Yes, he thinks it might be trouble with the main drain," said Lily. "How were your last X-rays?"

"I think they must be improving," said Harry. "Now whilst he's there will you ask him to look at that loose gutter near the back chimney. I've been worrying that it might fall on you and the kids one day." Yes, I thought, kill the bleeding lot of 'em and get 'em out of the way.

"Was your sputum test all right, Harry?" she said.

"They're waiting for the results. Are you managing all right? I mean, can you keep going?"

"Oh, that's all right. Yes, everything's going fine," she said. It had a dead hollow ring.

"I mean, about money?"

"I tell you we're all right."

"Are you sure?"

"Yes, certain."

"Did my mother come round?"

"Oh, yes."

"Was everything all right?"

"She seemed a bit put out because I hadn't made the kids a big cooked dinner."

"She's mad about Sunday dinners."

It's a pity she didn't give you a few more, I thought.

"I suppose she means well."

I couldn't bear to hear any more so I turned to Joe. "They're trying to get through to one another, Joe," I said, "but it ain't easy with their sort of mentality."

"I envy 'em," said Joe. "I'd swop places with him any

day in the week."

Here was a bloke retired, with any amount of money and I can see he means it when he talks about swopping places with Harry. So that shows how much money means.

"Know what, Joe," I said, "I ain't had a single visitor since I came in here. I keep 'em away – I tell them all I'm on silence."

"Why, who'd come to visit you?" said Joe. He was making out he was only taking the mickey, but I could see he meant it. "I tumbled you, Alfie," he said, "the first time I talked to you."

"Tumbled what?" I said.

"Do me a favour," he said.

"How do you mean, Joe?" I said.

"Never mind how I mean," he said. "I know your sort – all for number One. They'll wear it whilst you're your age – but wait till you get mine. You won't have a bleedin' friend in the world."

I thought he was coming it a bit strong. "Who – me?" I said, " – I've got more birds than – "

"I said *friends*," he said. "Know what, one woman came round to try and get me to go down to the Darby and Joan Club. 'You might find a Joan,' she said. 'I found my Joan forty years ago,' I told her. 'I don't ever want to find another.' "

"Ain't you never thought of going to live at the seaside, Joe?" I said. I don't mind talking about myself but I don't like others talking about me. I always say nobody understands you like yourself.

"What, on my own!" he said. "It'd be a living death. Besides, ain't you never seen one of those places in the winter? Another thing, I don't know how it is, but I can't get myself to make a will."

"Why's that, Joe?" I said.

"It's the way they start off – 'Last Will and Testament', as though you were going to die the next bleedin' minute. So same as I was saying, I'm nervous going off to sleep at night thinking who'll get all my money if I never wake up."

"But ain't you got a family, Joe?" I said.

"I've got one son," he said, "and he's a tearaway,

spendthrift and gambler. He'd go through that lot on women and dogs in no time."

"*Dogs*," I said, "then don't leave him nothing." I'm dead witty at times but nobody ever seems to notice it except myself. "I thought you had a daughter as well," I said.

"I have a lovely girl. But she's gone and got herself married to one of these Cypriots. I'm gonna see he doesn't lay hands on a penny of it. I ain't slaved forty years for his bloody benefit. Do you see my problem, Alfie? I've worked all my life, and I've got this money and it's a bloody millstone round my neck. I can't spend it and I've got nobody I want to leave it to." He looked in a right state did Joe.

"Why not leave it to Battersea Cats' Home?" I said.

"I would too," said Joe, "only I never cared for bleedin' cats either." He picked up his bag of apples and looked across at Harry and Lily. "Yes, I envy 'em," he said, "I envy the pair of them."

"But she'll go off in a few minutes and he'll be worrying all week long till he sees her again."

"Yes, but she's here now and he knows he will see her. He has something to look forward to. They both have. It's when you know you'll never see somebody again in this life, that's when it all feels hopeless – bloody hopeless."

CHAPTER THIRTEEN

I WATCHED old Joe totter off and the thought went through my mind what funny things human beings are. But what's the answer, that's what I keep asking myself. No matter which way you turn you're caught. I go through life with that question on my mind: what's the bleeding answer?

I see Lily take a letter out of her bag for Harry. As soon as I see it, I know it's a letter from their youngest kid, Phil, who's three years old. Now this letter is nothing but scrawls all over the paper. Yet I've often seen Harry take that letter up in his hand when Lily's gone and keep studying the scrawl. It was funny watching him there because that reminded me of this dream I had one night at the sanatorium. Stuck in my mind it did.

I find myself walking out in the middle of the road at night, see, in this dream when something suddenly comes down from the sky and blows up, and out of it come all these big round cans, what are every one exploding off, sending out loads of thick dust, see. Now it wasn't too bad, till I heard somebody shout out that it was the new bomb dust, that they'd just invented, see, the Japanese or Chinese, who were getting their own back on us, and I knew if one speck was to fall on you, you'd had it. So I thinks, I'd better get out of this lot, and I nips up the next road out of the way, where it was dead quiet and I'm the only one. This is lovely, Alfie, I says to myself, you were the lucky one again, and all the rest unlucky and just when I thought I was dead safe, one bleeding can came rolling round the corner, and came rolling up towards me, and suddenly it bangs off, and out comes this cloud of dust. So I dodges out of the way, and gets down on my hands and knees, at a house, knocking and banging on the door, see, shouting for them to let me in. I can see this new atom bomb dust is coming down, and if I don't get out of the way I'm going to be a goner. Then one geezer opens the door and I shouts at him: "Let me in! let me in, mate." And this bloke has no more savvy than let me in, so I crawls in on my knees. And as I do I sees some of this dust on my shoulder. But as luck would have it this bloke don't see it. And then behind him I sees a kid of three or four standing watching me, and suddenly it struck me who it was – it was young Malcolm. You know, what I told about earlier on – and I realised that like as not this dust on me would sooner or later kill the kid. And he's standing there so innocent. And I'm taking this dust to him – taking death to him, you could say. But what could I do? The thought struck me that I could crawl out, shut the door, and get back into the street. It would have been the thing to do. But even before the thought struck my mind I shut it out, if you see what I mean. I didn't want to know. I mean you don't want to know things like that, do you? You've got to

75

save yourself, I thought, and I did.

But I didn't half feel rotten when I woke up, and I said to myself: Alfie, if only you could get yourself to do something *good* in your dreams, it wouldn't cost you nothing, and you'd get quite a bit of satisfaction out of it. Of course it only goes to show – if they ain't got you when you're awake, they've got you when you're asleep. But what's the answer – that's what I keep asking myself.

Lily and Harry went on talking about drains, loose gutters and kids, and every in-between they'd just sit in silence, either looking at one another or looking straight ahead like two people you might see in a picture. It seemed dead painful to me at times when I gave a glance across at them to think how much their little hearts were in love with one another. Love is pain, ain't it. In twenty years' time, I thought, you'll hardly know one from the other. Well, you know how it is with these old married couples, they begin to look like one another. As a matter of fact I think we each one of us grow to look like that thing we love – that is, if we love anything at all. You've only to look at one of these old birds from Kensington as she's calling out to some horrible ugly pet dog, "Oh you naughty boy!" to see how much they look like each other. I once saw a bloke who bred bulldogs and I reckon he'd have taken first prize at any show. Still, some people would say it's better to love something than nothing.

Next thing into the ward comes this little ward orderly, Gina, a little Italian kid from a farm somewhere up in the mountains. I quickly slipped off my dressing-gown and got into bed. Well, you never know your luck. She's got a great bunch of big ugly flowers that Lily must have brought from the garden and handed in.

"Look what lovely flowers your wife brought you, Mr. Clamacraft," she said.

"Thanks very much," said Harry, and you'd think his face would split in two the way he keeps trying to smile his thanks to this Gina and then back again to his missus. And I'm just thinking they'll give him hayfever for certain – horrible dahlias, pompoms or something, which in my opinion are only meant for a hedge. Why women ever take flowers out of a garden I do not know, because if there's one thing I hate it's to see flowers around the place. I mean, you've no sooner put them in water than the petals are falling off, the water starts stinking, and you begin knocking them over.

"There's one lot for Mr. Elkins," said Lily, giving me one of her shy smiles.

"Yes, of course," said Gina, "I'll put them on his locker. Now don't let me disturb you, Mrs. Clamacraft," she said, "I know what it must be like only seeing each other once a week. Carry on as if I wasn't here. Some flowers for you, Mr. Elkins," she said, and puts these great dopy dahlias on top of the locker.

"Oh thank you!" I called to Lily, "Thank you very much." Then I saw her stoop and dip down into her basket and my heart sank.

"I've got a jar of home-made marmalade here for you, Mr. Elkins," she said. She handed the jar to Gina and Gina gave it to me. There were these big dark dollops of orange peel behind the glass and how anybody could eat that stuff I do not know.

"Home-made marmalade!" I said. "Why, that's fabulous! Thanks very much. That'll come in handy for breakfast."

Then she dipped down again and said, "There's a little jar of calves-foot jelly here if you'd like it – ?"

Calves-foot bloody jelly! I mean you never know where these calves' feet have been, do you – and even if they haven't been anywhere, they don't sound too good to me. How anybody can put something in a jar and call it calves-foot jelly and sell it, I do not know.

"You're spoiling me," I said.

She wasn't a bad little bird really, Harry's wife, only she'd never been handled right. Still, what I'm saying these things about people for. We've all got to find our way through life the best we can.

"Here," I said to Gina in a very loud voice, "ain't it time I had my injection?"

"Is it?" she said. "I'll go and tell Staff."

"Hadn't you better put the screen round?" I said. Then

77

I whispered. "It'll give *them* a bit of privacy, see."

She was in two minds, but then she did pull the screen round. They can talk about these boudoirs full of fancy mirrors, but give me a bed and a little Orderly or Nurse dressed in all this starched linen and smelling as clean as an apple. I mean for exciting certain things in a man. I hope that doesn't sound kinky. I never meant it that way. Old Harry and Lily went dead silent for a bit.

The first thing I heard him say was: "Are them crocus bulbs up yet?"

"They've started sprouting all over the place," Lily said. "Did I tell you about Rover when he got that big seed stuck in his ear?"

"No, do tell me," he said. "What happened?"

He's making out he's all ears – but the fact is he's facing Lily but he keeps turning his peepers towards the screen – I can see him through a slit.

"Well, I took him to the young vet – by the way, did you know that he's got five children?" said Lily.

"I didn't even know he was married," said Harry.

You wouldn't, I thought. I didn't hear the next bit or the bit after that. I didn't hear anything for a good minute – my mind was elsewhere – and the next thing I heard was Harry saying "What about young Phil?"

Now I knew he'd been thinking about him all the time, but he's that crafty he only begins to talk about it at the end.

"I can't tell you how much he misses you," said Lily, "he's not the same child. He seems to have gone so quiet. This morning he must have woken up early and I could hear him talking away to himself in his cot like he does. He kept saying 'Daddy' and it seemed he was scolding you."

The bell started ringing then and Gina got the screen out of the way. "Nurse will give you your injection after tea," she said to me.

"Tell Sister to send the Redhead," I said, "– the one who's a good dart thrower."

CHAPTER FOURTEEN

"THAT can't be the bell!" Harry said to Lily. You soppy git, I thought, you just heard it. "You seem like you've only just got here," he went on. "Don't go yet, wait for the others to go."

"I'll have to go, darling," she said, "or I'll miss the coach to the station."

I could feel the misery of those two across where I lay in bed. Thank God I'm not involved with anybody, I thought. Horrible ain't it, saying goodbye.

"You won't forget to write, will you?" said Harry.

"I'll write you a long letter the first thing in the morning," she said, "when they've all gone to school. I'll sit down and write before I clear the breakfast things, I promise you."

What the hell would she have to write about by tomorrow morning, I thought. And what does he want a letter for?

"Don't be frightened of putting little things in," said Harry. "You know, anything that strikes your mind. I mean like what Phil said when Rover was missing that night. I enjoyed that bit in your last letter."

"I'll put everything in," said Lily; "and be sure you write if you need anything special."

"Yes, I will," said Harry. "Give my love to the children."

"Are you sure you've got plenty of stamps?" said Lily.

"Oh I must have about half a dozen," said Harry.

"See you eat your eggs," she said. "They're special – from free-range hens."

"You will be careful, won't you!" he said.

I'm only telling half of it. On and on they went, about being careful, until the final bell sounded.

"I must go now, darling," she said.

"All right," said Harry. "Godspeed."

"God bless," she said.

And the next thing he's only broken out into a great fit of coughing, and you'd think he was going to choke. It's the way they have of drawing attention to themselves, see.

They can't help it. Anyway either I've got a soft heart or I'd had enough of it, but I got out of bed and slipped my dressing-gown on: "Come on now, Harry boy," I said, "easy up there. Breathe in and out slowly, and control yourself. You'll be all right. Your missus has to go."

He seemed to ease up at once when he heard me speak so firm to him. Lily looked at me, "I don't like leaving him!" she said.

"It was only a bout," I said. "Off you go, I'll look after him. He'll be all right." Know what, I sometimes think this world would be a happier place if all the sick people and whatnot dropped dead. When you get down to it they're only an encumbrance to themselves and everybody else.

"Thank you, Mr. Elkins," she said. "Do cheer him up if you can."

They clutched their sticky little hands together once more and she kissed him on top of the head, and I saw her off to the ward door. "Leave him to me," I said. "I'll give him a good talking to."

She went walking down the corridor. She looked a lonely little woman. They do, don't they. She hadn't a bad figure when you came to look at it closely – a bit homely, but none the worse for that. If she unloaded herself of that C & A coat, I thought, and got some proper clobber she wouldn't look too bad. She turned at the far end of the corridor and looked back and held up her hand and gave me a little wave. I didn't expect it. I turned up both my thumbs to her to tell her everything would be all right. Then off she went. She left a little spot of herself in my mind.

I went back inside the ward. Doris, the ward maid, was just wheeling in the teas. I felt badly in need of a cup. "There's a gal," I said. "I'll pour his out. Snaffle me an extra bit of bread an' butter if you will – I feel peckish."

"You can have mine," said Harry, " – I'm not hungry."

"Thanks," I said. I began walking about as I was eating. I think your stomach works better if you eat standing up. You can certainly talk better. "Now look here, Harry," I said to him, "I don't want to be hard on you – but these

80

visiting days aren't doing you no good. You've got to do something about them."

"How do you mean?" he said.

"It takes you a week to get over one," I said, knocking back his jam. "You know how you're going to leave here, Harry, if you go on like this – you're going to leave here in your wooden suit. Now why don't you write and tell your missus the doc's put you on silence."

"Silence?" he said.

"That's it," I said. "No visitors. Tell your missus not to come. Then you'll be like me, you'll have nobody to worry about but yourself."

He looked at me as though I'd gone mad: "It's the one thing I look forward to all week," he said. I could have understood it if they'd let her pop in between the sheets with him for ten minutes. I mean, that would have done him some good, but to sit there talking about drains and dogs and kids! What good could that do any man? He looked up at me with those big innocent blue eyes of his: "Alfie," he said, "I couldn't live without seeing Lily."

"Talk sense," I said, "you'd have to live without her if she was knocked down and killed on her way home. Or say she fell on the railway line in front of the train and crash" – and I demonstrated with my fist hitting up against the palm of my other hand what would happen to Lily if an express train hit her. I felt he needed a bit of shock treatment.

"Don't say things like that, Alfie," he said. "Not even in fun."

"I'm not being funny," I said. "Accidents do happen. Here, Harry," I went on, sitting down beside his bed and talking to him in a bedside manner, "how do you know she ain't got one geezer outside there waiting for her? I mean after all, you've been in here a good six months, ain't you, and in all that time she's not had a bit of cracker. She's only human like any other woman. You couldn't blame her."

"You say another word about my wife," he said, "and I'll get out of this bed and knock your bloody head in."

I looked at him and I realised he would have done if he

81

could. So that's what you get for trying to help people. It don't never do to give anybody advice. Those who are most in need of it are the least likely ones to take it.

"All right, all right, mate," I said, "don't get aeriated." What harm if she had, I thought – they say a slice off a cut loaf is never missed. Nor is it. And a woman's body needs to be kept fresh. I mean the old glands are very quick to pack in if they feel they're not wanted.

I went to Harry's locker and picked up his packet of cigarettes, since I'd smoked all my own. "Here you are, Harry," I said, "have a fag and cheer up. And I'll take one for myself at the same time if you don't mind."

He didn't know whether to take it or not. "The doc says I'm not to have more than five a day," he said.

"Take no bleedin' notice of the doc," I said. "You've got to get *yourself* better. He won't get you better. He can only advise you. But the real *get well* spirit must come from inside you. You'll get nowhere in this life, Harry, if you depend on others."

"I'll just have one," he said, "it can't do no harm."

"It'll do you *good*," I said. "Don't think of harm, think of good."

I got him smoking and generally cheered him up with my chirpy manner. Then I picked up the picture of his wife that he kept on his locker. "All I said to you was that you never know with a bird where it's been, or what it's done. And even when they're talking to you, Harry, they've got this skin over their forehead and these two eyes all covering up what's going on underneath." If many a man only knew what was going on inside his wife's head whilst he was talking to her, or even doing the other, what a bloody shock they'd get! "That's one thing you never will know – what a bird is thinking," I said. "It don't even know itself half the time."

"Would you mind saying *she*," said Harry. "You're talking about my missis."

"She or it," I said, "They're all birds. Just because she's your wife you think she's different but she's not." Old Harry looked at me as though I knew something, but not as much as he knew.

82

"What you don't understand, Alfie," he said, "is the bond between husband and wife."

"No, but what I do understand," I said, "is human bloody nature. All the birds ever made have to give way to that. You never want to let yourself get attached to anybody or anything in this life, Harry."

"Why not?" he said.

"If you're going to talk like that," I said, "I'm not going to tell you."

"I love Lily," he said.

"It doesn't follow you love somebody just because you're attached to them," I said.

"How do you mean?" he said.

"Here, I once knew an old woman, lived in Lambeth, an old spinster or something," I said, "what used to wheel a dog about in a pram. She had a little knitted shawl up to his chin, and as she was wheeling him about the other neighbours used to stop and chat to her and say 'How's Charlie this morning?' just as though he were a child. He used to look an ugly little sod, now I come to think of it. 'Oh my little Charlie's not so well this morning,' she'd say, 'Are you Charlie love?' This is gospel, Harry, every word of it. I remember chatting her one day and she said to me, 'I've lost my husband, so I've got to have something to take his place. Little Charlie sleeps on my bed and he's better company than any husband. He knows every word I say as I'm talking to you. He costs me twenty-five bob once a month to have him done over at the dogs' place at Stockwell. He has cornflakes for breakfast and boiled chicken for lunch. Don't you Charlie, love? It takes more to keep him than it does myself, but little Charlie is worth every penny of it – he's my own dear boy. I wouldn't part with him for all the money in the world'."

"She sounds a nice old dear," said Harry.

"Listen," I said, "just as she's having this good rabbit about little Charlie, some kids are going by with their mongrel dog that was yapping and barking away and suddenly this little Charlie spots him and he jumps clean out of his pram and joins in. Now the old woman started a-screaming her head off. 'He'll strain his heart,' she kept shouting, 'somebody stop him!' And there was her little Charlie chasing this mongrel up and down the street, and he was having the time of his life. Now when she got hold of him she didn't half scold him, and she put him back in the pram and covered him up to the chin and wheeled him off. I turned away from Harry. "She was like you, Harry," I said, "she wanted the dog to have a good time – but only with her."

"How do you mean?" said Harry.

"I mean if Lily was having it off with a bloke you'd feel –"

"Get on with your bloody tale," said Harry.

"Where was I? – oh yeh, the next thing the old woman falls down stairs and has to go into hospital, where she soon snuffs it. 'What will Charlie do now?' they all said. 'It'll break his heart,' they said. 'He'll never survive without her.' Know what, Harry, that dog took on a new lease of life when it got the old woman out of the way. It became young and frisky you wouldn't think it was the same dog. And people will still tell me she was devoted to her dog!" I picked up a little bunch of Harry's grapes. "You don't mind if I help myself to your grapes, Harry?"

"Carry on," he said, "I won't eat them."

" 'Devoted! devoted,' I used to say, 'she was devoted to her bleedin' self. The same as everybody else is.' I reckon if you're devoted to somebody the best thing you can do for them is to get out of their bleedin' way and let them stand on their own two feet."

"Don't talk daft," said Harry. "If people did what you say, we'd all be alone in this life."

"We are alone in this life, Harry," I said, "if you could only see it."

"Speak for yourself," said Harry. In a way I suppose he had me there, but he didn't follow it up. Nice bloke Harry. "And what about man and wife?" he said.

"It's all the same," I said, "– man, wife, or mother and son, or father and son, come to that. Now don't get depressed, mate, because once you see this truth – that man and wife ain't one but two, you'll organise your little life something lovely. You'll know the truth, see, and you'll be happy in the truth, mate, because you'll soon be out of here once you learn to live for your bleeding self like I do. See what I mean."

"I never worry about Lily," he said. "I'm the only chap she's ever had and I've no doubt I'll be the only chap she ever will have, even if I was in here another six years, let alone six months. But I do miss the kids, especially young Phil. I miss him a lot, Alfie."

"When you lie back in bed at night," I said, "do you start thinking about him? Do you start imagining what he's been doing all day and who he's been talking to?"

He looked at me quite surprised. "Come to think of it, I do," he said. "How did you know?"

"I've had experience," I said. I had too. Of course in time every memory wastes away. "A man should never allow too much from outside to get inside his nut. It don't do him no good. You've enough on your plate thinking about yourself. It sounds hard, mate, but that's only because the truth is hard. I'll bet you've been planning your little future lying back on that bed, but it don't do, Harry, because it only gives you the idea that what goes on in your head will one day come to happen. But it won't. It never does."

"How do you mean?" he said.

"I'll bet you've got the notion in your mind that your little family couldn't live without you," I said. "But suppose you was to snuff it tonight, Harry. See what I mean?"

Harry had a laugh. "Go on, mate," he said, "I can take it."

"I've got you giggling, Harry," I said. "You're halfway to being cured. That's all life is – a bleedin' giggle. But if you go taking it serious you're bound to come a cropper."

"Carry on with me kicking the bucket," said Harry. "Say it's happened – move on from there."

"There's my old son," I said. "Now say in a month or two your missis picks up with some new geezer and takes him home. Got me, Harry?"

"I don't think Lily would," said Harry.

"Off you go again," I said, "refusing to see reality. She ain't bad." I pointed at Lily's picture on his locker. "She's got a fair little figure, Harry," I said. "It might look nothing to you because you're used to it. And I'll admit it ain't

85

exactly my cup of tea – it's a bit on the staid side, if you see what I mean?"

"I see," said Harry, "carry on."

"Well there's many a bloke getting on in years might fancy a wife like that, kids and all, a ready made family. Course I prefer the old do-it-yourself method. But you get a retired grocer say, or some old boy who's a widower and manager of a shoe shop, and if he's lonely and he likes kids he might go for a little set-up like your'n. He might even be a churchwarden or something –"

"Get down to the gory bit," said Harry.

"Nah, listen," I said, "he could be one of these blokes who would have liked a wife but didn't fancy the bed stakes, so he's not bent but he's a sort of uncle geezer. Got me, Harry?"

"I've got you," said Harry.

"Now let's say, Harry, let's say she goes round with him for a bit, and then takes him home and introduces him to the kids as their Uncle Donald. You're at peace in your grave, mate, so it's no skin off your nose. Now I'll bet them kids would get a real kick out of him."

"They might and they might not," said Harry. "But certainly not young Phil."

"He'd be the first," I said. "He's missing his Daddy, he'd be longing to find another. That's a child's nature. Now say this Uncle Donald wants to make an impression he's going to take your kids some toys and chocolates. I'm not depressing you, am I, Harry?"

"He wouldn't buy young Phil with toys and chocolates," said Harry. "No, you're not depressing me."

"Good. Now the next thing your missis will start telling people, the kids have got to have a dad. Women always put it on to the kids. They won't come out with it straight and say, I've got to have a man about the house. No, the kids have got to have a dad, that's what they say. Like as not the kids will have settled down dead peaceful and happy without a man in the home. Kids don't like men around as a rule."

"What are you getting at, Alfie?" said Harry. "Come out with it straight."

"I'm getting at nothing," I said. "I'm only trying to get you to see life, mate. Once you do that the road's clear for you to start getting better."

I felt he needed a good shock to stir him out of himself. In fact we all do. "The wife and kids might go along to the cemetery every Sunday with flowers for the first month or two," I said, "– unless she decides it might work out cheaper in the long run to have you cremated. At least you get rid of the whole bloody lot in two seconds with that game – but once she's married again, and the kids are calling Uncle Donald, 'Dad', they'll stop thinking about you, and that little grave of your'n will be just a mass of weeds, with an old broken Woolworth's vase in the middle. Yes, Harry, you'll be totally forgotten by your little family, except for the odd time in the night when old Lily can't sleep or something, and she gets this odd little touch of memory about you – with this Uncle Donald lying beside her – and like as not she'll shed a tear or something in the dark." Harry was looking a bit tense, but once you've got the picture glowing in your mind you can't stop just for the sake of somebody's feelings.

"But as for you, Harry," I said, "if you was to walk into your own kitchen six months later, they'd all run to him and shout, '*Daddy – who is it? Send him away!*'"

I thought Harry could take it, but the fact is people can't. Nobody can. Harry was already trying to get out of bed to lay hands on me. It's better never tell anybody anything. "What's up, Harry," I said, "what's up?"

"You're trying to poison my mind," he shouted.

I very gently pushed him down again. "You're poisoning your own," I said. "Just ask yourself, Harry, if what I've just told you ain't the truth. Another thing, once you get used to it it ain't too bad. Take one good gulp and swallow the bleeding lot." I could see he already had an idea that it was the truth, but there was no getting him to swallow it. I'd had to but somehow others won't. "All I asked you, Harry, was to try to see life – what it is and what it does to you. Then no matter what happens to you, at least you get a giggle out of it. You don't start bleedin' moaning."

When I saw his white sweaty forehead and this unhappy

lad's eyes, I was sorry I'd spoke. It's my one trouble – I will keep going on after everybody's heard enough.

CHAPTER FIFTEEN

WHEN the train shunted into Waterloo Station and I stood up and got my suitcase down, I felt I'd have given anything to get back to my little bed in the sanatorium. It had never struck me the din around you every minute of the day in London, and it seemed to me that the porters and everybody, and the blokes driving the little trucks, were all deliberately making as much as they could. It made me feel dizzy. On top of this there was all the filth and dirt around. I don't mean just on the ground or on everything you touched, I mean in the air. I felt I didn't want to breathe. When I used to spit out in the country it was lovely and clean, but I remember that first spit I made when I was walking out of the station, it was as black as could be. Well, getting on that way.

I'd always been looking forward to the day when I'd leave the sanatorium, but same as everything else you look forward to, it turned out different. For one thing I'd made myself quite useful round the place, not only in helping serving the morning tea and that, but in one or two other handy ways. There were one or two fair little ward maids and orderlies about the place. This little Gina hadn't been very forthcoming at the start, but I had found it a nice little challenge. I quite enjoy working on a sulky bird providing the sulky streak hasn't got too firm a hold. If it has, the only thing to do is give 'em a kick up the backside and forget it. She was short and thick set – I might as well put you into the picture proper – with thick fingers and a thick little body, and she smelt a bit of garlic or something from the sausages her mum used to send her from the little farm up amongst the mountains. Here, don't get the wrong impression about these foreign girls that they're easy. Little Gina was one of the hardest nuts I ever had to crack. It needed constant patience and persistence. But once I set myself out to do a thing I don't like giving up – I mean halfway. She was very homesick for her mum and brothers and sisters and her little home so far away – and I played on that. I didn't give her sympathy, or any of that flannel, that would have been a mistake. I made out that I was lonely too – twin-souls, see. Well, you've got to do something.

In a way I think she helped me to get better. There's only one way to get over this T.B., or most other complaints come to that: don't take too much notice of the doc. Just listen to him to get the form, and then go your own way about getting better. It was always the patients who did everything they were told, who rested themselves, who didn't exert themselves, who took all the medicines, who stayed behind in the sanatorium when the others had gone away.

I felt so ribby the first few days back in London; that I had to tell myself that if I wasn't careful I would soon find myself back in the sanatorium. It's one thing wishing you were somewhere, and it's another being there when you get there.

Sharpey, this mate of mine, had found a little place for me next door to where he was living, with two little rooms and a kitchen and bits of furniture. Now for a start I had no interest in anything. It was all I could do to go and get myself to sign on and draw the National Assistance. It's very handy is that, and once you've started getting something for nothing you'll find it's not easy to break off the habit. Now whilst I was in the midst of all this gloom I suddenly said to myself: Alfie, you've got to take more interest in yourself; you've got to get up early tomorrow morning and go out and tackle life. Now same as I say, once I set my mind on something I'm not easily put off.

What I decided would now be my main concern in life – more so than money, birds, suits, a car, or anything else – would be my good health. After all, you can't enjoy any of the others to the full unless you've got your good health. Now the only way to go about it, I found out, is to have a routine.

For a start it's no use having a routine if you're going to let anybody get in the way of it. You must always put yourself and your own interests first if you want to get anywhere in this life. Now that might sound selfish to some people, but in fact it's one of the basic rules of life. If you're going to let anybody put you off what you aim to do you'll end up a failure. You'll find people are never happier than when they can stop you from doing what you've set your mind on. On top of that, if they can only get you to join in what they're doing – which is usually wasting time, talking, boozing, complaining – you'll make their day for them. Now about people putting you off your stroke. You mustn't even let *yourself* put you off, if you see what I mean. After all, we are each one of us divided in two – one part of you wants to forge ahead, and another part of you wants to keep you back. Now back to the drill.

First thing in the morning when I got out of bed I'd get this hard friction towel, soak it under the cold tap, squeeze it out, and start rubbing myself down with it. That's for a good circulation, see, most important. It feels ice-cold for a start, but you soon warm up with this rubbing. In particular, you've got to give your parts a good dowsing, and sponging over with cold water. They thrive on it – tighten up beautiful they do. It contracts the blood vessels see.

Here, I mustn't forget, I'd always have the window open wide, top and bottom. You might get the odd cold – O.K. what about it. You'll get that in any case. Now after that I'd set about doing my Royal Canadian Mounted Police exercises. They're quite good they are. Bending and stretching, down on your stomach and whatnot. They take eleven minutes by right, but I found nine suited me better. Then I always finish off with a good two minutes deep breathing exercises.

Now the trouble with most people is that they don't know how to breathe. They imagine the art of breathing is filling your lungs; it's not – it's knowing how to *empty* them. If you empty your lungs out properly, right out, so there's not a spoonful of air left inside, your stomach goes down dead flat, and you can lift the top end of your body clean up, and you get this marvellous feeling of being about seven feet tall. And when you breathe in, of course you've got to fill that bottom part not the top part. That'll fill itself. Mind you, if you've got a fat belly, every time you breathe correctly means your lungs have got to shove that out or lift it up. Most fat people find it's not worth the trouble.

Now the worse you feel when you wake up the more you need this routine. Say your head feels very hot, you start off the day by putting it under the cold water tap. Say your limbs feel dead weak, you leave more water in the towel. Here's a handy tip – soak the towel in a basin of salted water overnight: it feels after like having had a swim in the sea. You must never give yourself time to think, turn to your routine like a blind man turns to his stick.

Now, soon as I've finished I've got the kettle on the go and I have a glass of hot water, always with some lemon juice squeezed in, and a bit of honey. That gives the old stomach a good rinsing out. Then I have a little light breakfast, say toast and tea, or it might be toast and coffee, because I find coffee goes better with this lemon flavour in the mouth. Just as it goes better than tea does with marmalade.

Now you get a wonderful feeling when you go out in the morning air after that little lot. You see people slouching about the streets, going off to work with fags in their mouths, coughing and spluttering; you even get these old chars doing the outside of doctors' houses always with a burn between their lips, and you begin to wonder what the world's coming to. I always imagine how they must look with their clothes off. As for their insides they must be unthinkable. Of course, I cut out smoking completely once I'd got out – and after a couple of weeks I couldn't think how I'd wasted all that money over the years on fags. The money I would have had if only I'd saved it. I've learnt how to walk properly, see, keeping my stomach in and my shoulders straight, but relaxed, so that after a bit you find it a real pleasure. Best thing ever happened me was that breakdown in my health.

On top of this I found out by accident that one of the most beneficial things I'd ever known was eating the hearts of raw cabbages. It tastes lovely does the little tight white heart of a fresh cabbage. All you do is chew away at it. They only cost a tanner a time. I'd often make a meal out of that and a bit of cheese. I stuck to beer because I think that plenty of fluid keeps your kidneys and waterworks in good shape.

Now same as I say, all this health routine isn't a blind bit of use unless it's backed up by putting yourself first. You'd be surprised how soon everybody gets used to it. Nobody expects more from you than you give them the impression you'll deliver. So if you're doing something with some others, playing cards or snooker, and you suddenly feel it's not doing you any good, and you feel like a change or a breath of fresh air, just walk out. Always do what suits you best. Never consider others – let them consider themselves.

Now some people seem to think the old nukky knocks you out, but that's not my experience. It's only blokes who *think* it's doing them harm it harms. It's my opinion it keeps you young. What knocks you out is getting no proper sleep, and having the windows shut tight, the room full of horrible fag smoke, and a bird breathing its used breath into you all night long. You take a look at some of these old queers, going on about seventy, who are full of interest about other men, and they don't look a day more than fifty. But you see the average married man of seventy, who's given up that side of his life, and he looks about eighty-five. They've got an interest, see, these bent old boys, and same as I always say, and interest not only keeps you going, but it keeps you young. Those old boys will always carry on right until the day they carry them off.

CHAPTER SIXTEEN

Now I'd decided about that time to set about getting a bit of money at one side, to go with my good health. To sort of back it up. I wasn't going to get over-ambitious or nothing like that, just a few hundred nicker at one side. Know what, I found it dead easy after the start. What you do to make money is to buy and sell; all you need is a bit of capital, and it's handy to have some luck. I found that if I'd had a car a week and somebody made an offer, I'd flog it for twenty or twenty-five quid profit. I bought watches and all sorts of things. If anybody had something to sell they'd nearly always turn to me and say: "Alfie, how much will you give me for this?" The marvellous thing is the difference between the value in something you want to buy and something you want to sell. If a working bloke's hard up he suddenly gets the notion that money's very scarce and he'll sell cheap, whereas if he's got a bit of money he never gets the notion that there's plenty knocking about and he'll buy dear. I never dealt in real hot stuff, though I'll admit some of it was warm. It's surprising how it mounts up if you're not paying income tax on it. I'd still do two or three days a week driving, just to keep my hand in and fill the time in. You've got to move around to know what's going.

Now to scrape up the money at the start, I was determined to do anything – provided, of course, it didn't interfere with my health. I didn't bother much about pleasure because I felt if you keep going, that'll work its way in.

For a start I did a little bit of black work as they call it – weddings and funerals, see, for one bloke I know who owned three cars. I'd get three nicker for the Saturday afternoon, all free of income tax of course, and bit of dropsy if I was lucky. My mate Sharpey had always knocked out an easy living without working, and I went out on a few jobs with him. I did a turn on the smudge in the Haymarket and at Tower Hill. I even worked Oxford Street with him for a day or two, flogging kids toys from a tray. You could make ninepence or a shilling a time selling these toy spiders. You demonstrate with one on the pavement and you keep jerking this thing in your hand and the spider runs about. Of course, what you need for all those jobs is what they call *a worker*. You've got this special one, but the one the kid takes home ain't going to be a bit like that. Same with balloons. You can get a worker you can blow up about five feet in diameter. Now, when a kid sees this he pesters his mum to buy one. Of course, when he gets back to Acton or Surbiton, or wherever it is, and he tries to blow that balloon up he bought, he'd better look out when it gets more than eleven inches because it'll pop off.

I'd quite a few of those jobs, but it's not really my line of work. Mind you, you can sometimes have a very good day. I remember going out to the races with Sharpey, and it seems there's a bent copper on the gate at one of the enclosures. Now admittance tickets are a couple of quid each, but Sharpey and his mates have straightened this copper so that every time they come out of the enclosure on the quiet they pass him a fiver. Of course, he keeps rabbiting that he wants more – he's got very big eyes this copper, and he can see they're making a lot and he wants a bit more of the gravy. Now, I'm outside and I'm flogging these pass-out tickets for a quid or ten bob a time, and they're going like hot cakes. There was another copper on the gate who wasn't bent, and he can't make out where all the mob was coming from with the pass-out tickets. Anyway, long before the big race was off you can't turn round inside that enclosure. The officials must have been baffled because there were about three or four of Sharpey's customers to one of the legals. We made a nice tenner a piece that day. Leastways I did – but Sharpey must have made a lot more.

It's quite a skilled little job being a good ticket tout, as they call them. You've got to look for what they call a *Face*. Nobody can tell you what it is that is different about this face from any other of the dozens of faces that are milling past you as you try to sell your tickets. But Sharpey was an expert in spotting one. The nearest I can describe it is a bloke who is going about without his defences up. That's the man to stop. What put me off was one time when I had three tickets for the England-Scotland match at Wembley, and I was fool enough to pull them out in front of some of these Scotties. They took the lot and were away before there was anything I could do. It sharpens your wits, if they need sharpening, but somehow I was glad to get back to doing a bit of driving. I feel better if I'm earning an honest penny.

CHAPTER SEVENTEEN

Now to get back to my little life. I'm doing very nicely on all this buying and selling caper, but same as I say, I like picking up any little job in between. Now on this occasion I'm doing this two-three days on private hire – no tax – with an old Daimler, and I've got this little job driving two Japanese about. Lovely tippers are Japanese, they used to slip me a couple of quid at the end of every day. The worst tippers are Germans. I find Americans dead mean, too, except for the odd one, and he makes up for the rest. By the way, I was beginning to feel real good now. I'd both my lungs working full blast, and I wasn't knocking myself out too much one way or another. I mean except for occasionally.

This day I've took these two geezers out Hertfordshire way, where they'd fixed up to have a round at golf with two English blokes they're buying machines off, or selling machines to – I never quite made out – and they simply couldn't get the balls in the holes. I mean the Japanese pair. I've never seen anything like it. Anyway one of these blokes fixes up that he'll take my two back to town in his Jag so that I'm left to freewheel back just as I like.

So along the drag I stop and call in at this transport caff called Flo's. I used to look in there quite a bit in the old days. It's a quiet time, about eight o'clock, just going dark, and there's hardly anybody in. Now I'm chatting this Flo up, and she's standing behind the counter making bacon and egg sandwiches and handing out tea, when in walks this driver Lofty with a mystery in tow. I spots it at once and it takes my fancy. One of these quiet-faced birds who don't say much but you feel there's a lot going on underneath. Lofty is carrying the suitcase, which he puts down beside it at a quiet little table. Then he comes up to the counter.

"Hy, Lofty," I said.

"Egg an' chips, twice, Flo, doubles, and put a couple of sausages on if you've got any," he said to Flo. "How're you going on?" he said to me.

"Hearty but poor," I said. It's a funny thing, but if I'm talking to anybody, I find I begin to talk their way. If I meet a Welshman I go all sing-song.

"Right, Lofty," says Flo. "Bread and butter?"

"Two lots, please. I'll take the two teas now, one large, one small."

"Who's the young lady, Lofty?" said Flo.

"Her name's Annie," said Lofty, "she's from the North."
He turned round and looked at the table and she gave him
a shy smile back. I could see she wasn't one of the road girls.
Then a bloke called Lacey comes in and takes a good look
at this little Annie and comes up to the counter.

"Who's the mystery?" he says. "I ain't seen it around
before."

"She's no mystery," says Lofty.

"Is it yours, Lofty?" says Lacey. "Where d'you lap it
up?"

"I didn't lap it up," says Lofty. "I gave the young lady
a lift from Bury. Anything more you'd like to know?"

The way Lofty gives Lacey a look shuts Lacey up for the
time being. Then Flo says, "She's got a real sad look about
her. She ain't in trouble is she, Lofty?"

"Not yet," says Lacey.

Lofty gives Lacey another look. "That'll be enough from
you, mate," he says. This Lofty isn't a geezer to get on the
wrong side of. Actually he's a decent bloke, and you can't
blame him being a bit sharp, because it makes you edgy if
you've got a bird in tow and they've all got big eyes for her.

"I didn't mean it that way, Lofty," says Flo. "I just meant
she looked unhappy."

"Small tea and a bit of cake, Flo," says Lacey. He watches
Lofty going back to the table with the teas. "Old Lofty is
getting very possessive," he says.

"It's the first time I've seen him bring a girl in," says Flo.

"Here, I picked one up last Friday night," says Lacey,
"near Jack's Castle. It waved me down it did and when I
stopped it couldn't get into the cab – its skirts were that
tight, see. I had to go out and lift it in, just like it were a
bleeding mummy. The same when it was getting out."

The door opened and in came this mate of mine called
Fatchops.

"Hy, Alfie," he said. "What are you doing here? You're
not back trunking are you?"

"What, in this get-up?" I said. "Nah, I'm doing a turn
on the private hire."

"I believe Sharpey had you working the smudge with him," said Lacey.

"What's the smudge?" said Flo.

"The old street photographer's lark," said Lacey.

"I did a week on it," I said, "but then the rain killed it."

"I expect you'd pick up plenty of cracker on that game," said Lacey.

"The odd bit," I said.

Matter of fact, come to think of it, I'd got myself a marvellous bint called Ruby. She's a mature woman, see, a woman who's got on in life, and she's in her early thirties and quite mumsie, very warm and generous upstairs if you see what I mean. Not fat, mind you, but solid. Here, when I first laid hands on this Ruby I definitely knew I'd got hold of something. And when she ran her fingers over me I could feel a lifetime's experience in them. She's what you call a career woman and she's been very successful at it. Only owns three hairdressers' shops and got her own flat on the sixth floor overlooking the river in a block called Thompson Court. Admitted it's a bit poncey, what with porters and one thing and another, but she's got a cocktail cabinet, a big refrigerator, a Colston dishwasher, a twenty-one inch telly, handsome thick red carpet and mirrors you can see yourself in all over the place. In fact she's almost too good for me – with a set up like that.

Now I've still got my eye on this bint that's come in with Lofty. It's the sort of bird nine out of ten blokes won't even see, but it's got this waiflike look, and I find I often go in for that sort of thing, because a bird like that only needs drawing out of itself, and there's often a hidden treasure underneath. Besides which they're inclined to be more appreciative and much less demanding.

Lofty was trying to put her at her ease in his clumsy way, offering her fags, but it seems she doesn't smoke. That says something in her favour, I thought. Then he came up to the counter for the grub.

"They're almost ready," said Flo. "I'm putting you grilled tomatoes on, o.k.?"

"Eh? Oh sure, sure Flo," said Lofty. He's just that bit

slow on the uptake. Flo put both plates on the counter.

"It's going to be a checkbook order," said Fatchops.

"I don't mind," said Lofty.

"Where d'you pull it, Lofty?" said Fatchops "– and don't tell me it's the landlady's daughter."

"I didn't pull *it*," said Lofty, "I gave the young lady a lift from Bury. Owt else you want to know?"

"Yes," said Fatchops. "Is that your load outside with the pre-fabs or chicken houses or whatever it is they are on?"

"Yeh. What about it?" said Lofty.

"Well it was just coming on heavy rain when I came in," said Fatchops, "and I thought that the bloke whose load that was, was going to have a hell of a job with it if he didn't loosen up his loading ropes on account of the wet."

"Ta mate," said Lofty, "I'll attend to it."

I was going to say that he'd better not forget or else he'd have a load of trouble later but I didn't because I thought it might make him suspicious, which he'd have been quite right to feel. So he goes back with the two platefuls of grub to this little bird sitting at the table. Then when one or two drivers join in the chat about what things can happen to your load in wet weather if you get your ropes shrinking and they pull your load to one side. Then this leads on to one chap telling about a load of sheepskins he'd had and how they began to slip. Of course another driver has to top this with how he's going up the Shap in winter with fifteen ton on and he has to stop and the whole thing starts slipping back.

Now if there's one thing gets on my wick it's drivers talking about their wagons and their jobs. All an engine is to me is a block of metal under a bonnet, and its only purpose, so far as I can see, is to get you from one place to another. So there I was joining in but not taking a blind bit of notice and thinking to myself what a pity it was I didn't have any company for my little ride back to London, whilst here is this quiet little bint noshing it away with Lofty.

Anyway he gets his grub down in record time – he's got a terrific twist on him – and tells his lady companion that he's

98

going out to ease off his loading ropes. At least that's what it looks like to me the way he's talking to her and the signs he's making with his hands. He's a very slow thinking sort of bloke and talks to you like you were deaf and dumb. Now when I see him go off I say: "This place is getting into a real clutch-and-gear-joint. I think I'll go across and have a little tune on the old juke box to brighten things up."

Now as luck would have it the juke box chances to be up against the table where this Annie is sitting all on her todd. So I look down the list and I happen to remark, more to myself than to her, "Blimey, they've got a load of old 'uns on here."

I looked out of the corner of my eye to see what its reactions are and it gives me a little smile. It looks dead lonesome in its own little way. "Did you come in with Big Lofty?" I said.

I've only watched her come in haven't I. But I find that a very good approach with a bird to say something dead ordinary at the start. It wasn't well timed because she's chewing a mouthful of sausage so that all she can do is give me a nod. Still it makes it think maybe I'm not so bright. Always keep your best lines tucked away for the right occasion.

I keep on looking down the list of records because a bird like that is like a child, they're soon overfaced if you go for them, you've got to let them come to you. So without turning to it I start singing Lofty's praises. "He's a good bloke is Lofty," I said, "a real good mate, one of the few drivers you can rely on in these days. He'll never let you down. You're in good hands with Lofty."

"Yes, he seems nice," she said.

"Oh a good hearted geezer is Lofty," I said. "He'll give you anything. He'd share his last cigarette."

"Yes, he seems generous," she said, a nice smile coming to her eyes.

"He's his own biggest enemy," I said, "he'll even share his girl friends with his mates." I took a gander at her and another through the window at old Lofty who I could just make out going round his wagon easing off his ropes in the dark. "I suppose I'm fussy, but I never fancy that sort of game," I said. "One bloke told me that he'd even lend you his wife, like the Eskimos do – I wouldn't fancy a thing like that, for one thing she's as big as he is –"

"– I didn't know he was married," she said.

"Oh he's got at least one wife," I said, "being a trunker, see, a long-distance driver, away from home every other night. They usually have a wife at home and the landlady or her daughter at their digs. Well you can't blame them. It's not the sort of life I'd fancy. What was I saying now? – here, but aren't some blokes funny, I'd hate anything like that, sharing a bint – I mean a gal. Where are you making for, Annie?"

"London," she said. "How did you know my name?"

"Lofty was talking about you," I said, "Where are you making for in London?"

"Well no particular part, I'd like to get a place to stay and a job if I could," she said.

"Don't stay at one of these hostels whatever you do," I said. "You get an odd class of women in there, you know the sort I mean. You've got to look after yourself. What kind of job?"

"I don't know," she said. "I've worked mostly as a packer in a mail order firm."

"What kind of males?" I said. Same as I always say, you've got to make 'em laugh a bit. "Here I might be able to help you," I said. "I've got a mate who's a foreman at one of these sweet factories in London. You can earn about fourteen quid a week and come out with your pockets full of toffees."

"Oh how nice," she said. "Could I see you there?"

"I could run you down there," I said. "I've got a car standing out there, a Daimler with heater, radio, the lot. Come on if you're ready. Finish your sausage."

"Oh but I'd have to tell the driver who went out first," she said.

"Don't take that risk," I said, "he'd knock your block off, mine too come to that. He's a very funny tempered geezer. Listen, can you see that door there, well if you go out by that door you'll come out at the back. Now about fifty yards down the road you'll see a phone kiosk, slip off and wait for me there."

"Oh I couldn't do that," she said. "Not go off and leave someone who had been so kind to me."

I took another peep through the window and I could see Lofty was almost done roping up. "If you tell him he'll never let you go off with me," I said. "Now don't be frightened of me, gal, I ain't a wolf, I won't do you no harm." What ever I might do to a bird I don't seem to frighten it – and what ever I might be I'm not kinky looking. It's not just being fresh faced it's the look in your eyes. "You'd better make your mind up, gal," I said – "you don't want sharing, do you?", and I put my hand in front of her face with three fingers sticking up.

She looked up at me, and then at my three fingers, and then she picked up her bag and made out by the sidedoor I'd told her to go by. I had the tanner in my hand ready to pop into the juke box in case Lofty should have turned up unexpectedly, so now I pushed it in and pressed the number of the knob for the record I wanted. Out came blaring an old tune called the Tennessee waltz. I knew there was no time to waste, so I slipped across and paid Flo. Lacey and Fatchops had tumbled me and they warned me what Lofty would do if ever he laid hands on me. I nipped out the proper door just as he was coming in. "Everything all right, Lofty?" I said.

"Eh? – oh sure, sure everything's all right," he said. I could just hear the record on the juke box *My friend stole my sweetheart away*. I nipped across and into the car, started up and raced off down the road, where I could see this little bird called Annie standing so pathetic with her holdall in her hand beside the telephone kiosk.

CHAPTER EIGHTEEN

It's come Sunday morning round and there's a bit of sunshine coming through the kitchen window, and I'm at the kitchen sink, see, having a good scrub down, a top-and-tailer as they call it, and if there's one thing I enjoy it's having a good scrub and swill down of a Sunday. Preferably with an old towel on the floor under my feet. To be quite frank, I always feel a lot cleaner after a good sluicing down at the sink than I do if I have a hot bath. I mean you get into a bath and with all that water coming up under your chin you get a feeling you could easily drown; on top of which when you stand up all the dirty scum on top of the water goes onto your body again.

I find I'm not going in for these cold salt-water rub downs the same since little Annie came to stay with me. And it's the same with my Royal Canadian Mounted Police exercises. Well, the fact is, you can easily become a crank if you don't watch yourself, with all that exercise and cold water. I'll admit you feel better for it, but Annie seems to have got me into the habit of an early morning cup of tea. Well, I reckon you can't beat it, I mean give yourself a bit of comfort in this life.

As I'm drying myself I look through the door into the next room and there it is, down on its knees scrubbing away, and to be quite honest, and though I say it myself who shouldn't, it hasn't come up bad. Its little face looks quite content as it scrubs away, its hair's come up quite nice after washing – I mean, you never see the natural colour of a woman's hair in these days with all these tints and bleaches, but Annie's hair has come out auburn or whatever they call it, and its little skin has come out in a nice little glow too.

It's quite dainty, and I no sooner take off a pair of socks than it washes them – the same with shirts. It doesn't allow things to pile up. There's nothing a man enjoys more than seeing a woman slaving away for him. I suppose what it boils down to is that at heart every man is a bit of a ponce. 'Course you'll never get one of them to admit it. Sometimes I think it's a bit too quick. I mean you don't want a bird grabbing your socks the minute you take them off and washing them. You begin to wonder what's behind its mind.

Of course it's turned my little gaff into a palace compared with what it used to be. It can cook too, bit limited on the menu, goes in mostly for Lancashire hot-pot, Irish stew, and steak-and-kidney pudding – they blow you up a bit – but it do make a marvellous egg custard. Three eggs to the pint of milk, sugar, a twist of lemon peel, and a couple of hours on a very low flame in the gas oven with a grating of nutmeg. I've never tasted anything like it. It's quite fair on the other too. It's a bit on the shy side, and it would never make the first move, but I find all that quite a change in these days.

As I stop drying myself and watch it, and it doesn't know it's being watched, I can see it almost talking to itself as it listens to this old record it's got playing away on the record-player. "*I know that one day you'll want me to love you, when I'm in love with somebody new.*" What a bleeding hope, I thought, as I watched it. I had a feeling to go up to it and say: "Annie, why don't you grow up – or bleeding waken up, and tell him to get stuffed, whoever he is." But I didn't. I find as I'm getting older I'm getting more considerate. Anyway, it don't do to take away a bird's daydreams if you ain't got new ones to put in their place. If it's a crumb of comfort to it, I thought, what harm!

I knew it was in love with some geezer. I knew from the day I took it in. In fact I knew from the first look I gave it. And I know all this scrubbing and cleaning and cooking it's doing is only to keep him out of its mind. Now I'll ask any man something: which would you sooner prefer, to have a bird slaving away for you, cooking, cleaning and scrubbing and even sleeping with you, with another bloke in its heart – or to have a bird around all day and night who never stops telling you how much it loves you but is too bleeding stupid to boil a kettle? Do you see what I mean?

I give myself a good going over with Yardley's Eau-de-Cologne for Men, with a good rubbing up of the deodorant stick under my arms – I do love to smell fresh I do – and I watch Annie, *scrub, scrub, scrub*. It takes some birds like that. Not all of them, in fact very few in these times, they seem to mope about more rather than work it out of their systems. Here, I had a bird at one time, a great big fat thing it was, called Iris, got crossed in love or something – well the bigger they are the heavier they fall – used to sit in front of the fire all day smoking Park Drive and drinking tea, its shins burnt red raw. So one time I called out to it "Give's a cup of tea, Brackenshins." So it looked up at me and it said: "What, you bleedin' paralysed?" Know what, I had a hell of a job throwing it out. They're like cats in that respect – if they find a cushy gaff they never want to move.

"You've made a lovely little job of this shirt, Annie," I said. Terylene and Egyptian cotton mixture and it's my opinion you can't beat it – drip-dry of course but always come up better for a touch of a not too hot iron.

"I'm glad you like it," said Annie, smiling up at me. "Are you going visiting your friend at the sanatorium?"

"Old Harry? Yes, I thought I would." I looked down at it wringing out the mop in the bucket and I don't know whether I'm getting soft-hearted or something but I heard myself say: "Do you fancy a run out, gal?"

She looked up at me and I got a feeling that she had sensed I'd been a bit hasty in asking her. I might be wrong, of course, it might have wanted to stay home. "I've some washing to do," she said.

"You've never done washing," I said, "why don't you rest yourself a bit?"

"I feel better if I'm doing something," she said.

"If it makes you feel better, gal," I said, "I ain't going to stop you." Never stop a woman from working. If you do you'll get her frustrated. It was punishing itself, see, then life couldn't get at it the same. Poor bloody women, they don't half suffer one way or another, but what can you do? You can't argue with nature. They seem born to suffer.

"Alfie, what time will you be back?" I heard her ask.

Now, if there's one thing I hate it's a bird asking me – or anybody asking me, come to that – what time I'll be back, before I've even gone out. "I've told you never to ask me that, haven't I, Annie?" I said. "When I go out that door I don't even know what day I'll be back let alone what time. I'm what you call a free agent."

"I know that, Alfie," she said, "but I just thought it would give me the chance to have a nice meal ready."

"Make one of those meals that's always ready," I said, "you know, a stew or an 'ash or something." With a woman you've got to make it clear at the start what comes first – her meals or your freedom. If you don't you'll never have a minute's peace when you're out. Nothing a woman loves more to tyrannise a man with than the table.

"I thought I'd do something special," she said.

I felt a bit humpty as I began to put my tie on – to think that little Annie could start asking that – when I'd be back. A chance remark like that could be the writing on the wall – and we'd been so cosy those few weeks. It's not what a woman says you've got to take into account – but what's behind her words. They never say a thing in the way a bloke takes it. They're deep I tell you, very deep are women.

Mind you, I hadn't taken little Annie straight in and set her up living with me after lapping her up that time from Lofty. What I had done was this. I took her to my gaff, but I didn't take any advantage of her or put her under any obligation, because if there's one thing takes the edge off my enjoyment it's the feeling that a bird is doing it because she feels obligated to you. I mean, I could've started something in the car, couldn't I. Same as I say, it's only a Daimler, big seats, a heater, everything, but I didn't. Why not? I don't know.

We went the two of us very quietly into my place and I carried her little hold-all bag for her, but any gentleman would have done that. Now, the first thing I did when I got her into the room, well, not the very first, but next door to it, I pointed to the bed and I said, "This is my bed, Annie, but if you want to come in with me, you're welcome. And if you don't want to come in with me, you're still welcome – you can sleep on that little sofa. To be quite frank I sleep better on my own but if you want to come in, come in. Anyway, by the looks of you you'll want a little wash and whatnot just to freshen yourself up. I've got some lovely soap – costs two and threepence a tablet – and you're welcome to use that. I'll make a nice pot of tea, and I can promise you you won't be disturbed or looked at over your toilet.'' All nice and civilized, see.

So little Annie has this wash and I make this pot of tea and some toast. Another thing, I put some clean sheets on the bed. Now that's a handy little tip – whatever else you haven't got, always have an extra pair of clean sheets at one side: you'd be surprised how handy they come in. Then I made up the sofa for Annie. Here, now that's a funny thing – I'll tell you why – what with heating her water, letting her use my soap, making her tea and whatnot, something I hadn't realized began to come into it. *I was looking after her.* She was a little guest under my roof, you could say. So there, you never want to start waiting on a bird and looking after her if she's in your gaff. Let her find her own way about. Otherwise you'll find the mood changing, same as it did with me until it seems like liberty-taking to sleep with her after that.

So same as I say, I put her down to sleep on the sofa – I couldn't tell some of my mates that – but about four to five in the morning, and the light from the street lamps has gone out, and that cool light you get at dawn has come sneaking in, well anybody can feel a bit ribby if they're awake at that hour. So I chanced to wake up and I could sense Annie was wide awake. She was lying dead still and her eyes were closed but you can always tell whether somebody's asleep or not. So I called across to her: "Hy, mate, why don't you come in beside me?" Now she hesitated. She hesitated for about two full seconds, as though she was working it all out in her mind, then she got up and came in beside me. Somehow I find love has got a more tender flavour to it about that hour of the morning, dropping in as it does, quite sober, between one lot of dreams and another.

Now, comes the morning – things always look different by the morning light – I told her after we'd had our cup of tea that I had to go off and do a day's grafting. I explained that she'd have to come out with me as I couldn't leave her behind. Safety first.

I'd once let a mystery stay the night with me, and out of

kindness left it in bed when I nipped off at nine a.m. to do this little job collecting the effects of a gent's wardrobe from one geezer's widow in Montague Square, W.1., who had flogged them to a dealer I know. And so I'd given it the warning – this bird I mean, – it came from Nottingham, the city of lace – to be up and have breakfast ready by eleven a.m. when I'd be back. After all it had swore its undying love during the night, three or four times in fact. Breakfast! – it's only blown – blown and took with it most of the effects of *my* wardrobe – three suits, four shirts and all my ties. So after that little experience I've learnt my lesson and I've turned Annie out for the day, ain't I, telling her I'll be back at five o'clock, and if she hasn't found a better kip she's more than welcome to return. Same as I say, you must get things on a proper business-like footing with a bird at the start – let them know where they stand – or you'll mislead them, and end up bad friends. And I hate anything like that. I turned her out and sure enough she's there waiting for me at five o'clock. The same the next day. So on the third day I took a risk, I thought what the hell, and I left her in possession. Though naturally I locked her in. I mean I ain't all that trusting.

I could hardly believe my eyes when I got back and opened the door. It had transformed my little gaff. I'd never realised what the colours of things were under the dirt. It had cleaned the windows, washed the curtains and scrubbed the kitchen, and it looked dead happy after all its exertions. I always say a happy woman is a woman you find work for. Providing, of course, you see she does it.

I went on dressing and thinking when I heard it dowsing the floor-cloth into the bucket of sudsy water. "Annie," I said, "why don't you wear those rubber gloves I bought you – the yellow ones? You'll ruin your hands with all that scrubbing and whatnot."

She looked up at me and gave me one of her pale smiles: "They don't matter, Alfie," she said.

"They might not to you, gal," I said, "but they do to me." Nothing puts me off more than a woman getting hold of me with hard, horny mitts. Or stroking my face with that kind of hard, dry, shiny skin they get from keeping on washing-up. I'm very touchy about those sort of things. I stooped down over her and took hold of her hand. "Those are real pretty fingers you've got, Annie," I said, "they're like a child's. Do look after 'em for me." Then I kissed her hand and kissed her cheek. After all it's little enough to ask. I mean you shouldn't have to tell 'em. Know what, the sight of a woman's worn out hand can bring a lump in my throat.

I felt this little spasm of sympathy I sometimes get when I looked into her eyes. I thought of how the poor little thing gets this dead ghostified look creep over its little face, as if it was all sick and weary inside itself, if you see what I mean, with love or something, and its poor mind was stumbling about looking for a quiet corner to rest in. Love can be quite a horrible little thing once it gets itself knotted up inside a bird's heart.

Here, that reminds me of something. The night before, Saturday, Annie and I were together – you know what I mean – when I saw this tear or something on its cheek, and it opened its eyes and I spots a real far-away look there. It's not often I look into a woman's eyes at that precise time. Now I'm not a touchy bloke, I mean that up to a certain point I don't mind what a bird has on her mind, after all that's her business, but come certain moments and even I can get quite niggly. So I took my hand from between the sheets and I gave it a quick belt across the kisser. I don't know what made me do it, because I'm not the sort of bloke to raise a hand to a woman. I mean I'd sooner pack her in altogether than do that sort of thing. After all, you don't want to get that intimate that you're on striking terms. "Forget him, gal," I said. "I'm here and in the flesh." Come to think of it, I was. True enough she was only thinking, but after all, there's a time and place for everything, and even your thoughts have their proper place.

"Sorry, Alfie," she said, and her face came over real guilty. She'd a kind of oval face – you don't see so many of those sort of faces around on working girls. I was sorry I'd spoke. She looked upset at being found out. I said to myself: Alfie, she's as sensitive as you are! Yet no doubt the shock must have done her good.

"Annie, I'm nearly ready –" I said.

"I'll give you a brush down, Alfie," she said, "not be a tick." That's what I like to see – a willing woman. One volunteer is worth four pressed men. She wiped her hands and took hold of the clothes-brush and began to brush me down. That's the beauty of a gal like Annie, the light touch. I've had some birds brush me down and it's been like being birched in a Sauna bath – you're black and blue when they're through.

"Shall I say you'll be back about seven, Alfie?" she said.

"You can *say* what you want, gal," I said, "no harm in that. But whether or not I'll be back is another matter entirely. You have something ready and if I'm here I'll eat it, and if I ain't here I won't. It's as simple as that." You've got to make yourself clear with a bird – it's always on the watch-out for doubts. I didn't want to carry it too far because as soon as I get uppity it seems something brings me down.

"Know what, Annie," I said, "you're quite a nice looking gal, you are straight, only you need to brighten yourself up. You don't want to mope around scrubbin' and washin' and thing' all the time – thinkin' that's a way out. That's nearly as bad as anything else. You can dope yourself with work like some people do with drink. You want to shake yourself right out of it." That was as far as I wanted to go with what I knew about her. "So long, gal."

"Take care of yourself, Alfie," she said.

"Make yourself a nice little pot of tea," I said, "and get your feet up." I thought how that must be the only bird in my life I'd had to give that advice to.

"Yes I will," she said, "as soon as you've gone."

But I could see she wouldn't. She'd put that record on again, about the geezer who'd want her when she didn't want him, and she'd start scrubbing and polishing and washing all my socks and shirts. Still, I suppose we've all got to get through life the one way we know. You've got to have a bit of charity in your outlook on others.

CHAPTER NINETEEN

I DROVE off in this second-hand Vauxhall Velox I'd bought handy. You never want to buy a doctor's used motor-car, because they're in and out of the car all the time, out visiting patients, and though the mileage might be low on the clock, the doors and driving seat are worn out. You can always replace an engine but you can't replace them.

As I was driving over Lambeth Bridge the sun was shining and there was a lovely little view of Westminster and the City, so that even I stopped to have a look, and I thought what a cracking little place London is on a sunny Sunday morning.

It was a pity I'd had to leave little Annie behind, but of course I couldn't have taken her with me, because I'm off to visit this Ruby. I don't know any feeling much nicer than you're saying goodbye to one bird to go off to meet another. Whoever said a change was as good as a rest must have had birds in mind. It sort of re-charges all your batteries. Now Ruby's one of these women who go in for Sunday lunchtime drinks. It seems quite a number of these toffs go in for that sort of lark, having a few mates call in and knocking back these gin cocktails made up of Martini, then eating a few nuts and seeing 'em all off about half past one in the afternoon and going to bed with the *Sunday Express* and the *News of the World*. But she don't seem to want me to meet her friends, so she just makes it a party for two.

I got past the porter all right, and then went up in the lift to the sixth floor, and along the corridor to Ruby's flat. I rang the bell and waited. She always makes me wait. She thinks I don't know her game but I do. She likes to keep me in my place, see. For myself I would prefer not to mix with birds from a different station in life – because sooner or later they're going to let you see it – if they don't do it in touches along the way. I rang it pretty quick again and kept my finger on it. It doesn't do to let a bird go too far. She opened the door sharp: "What are you so impatient about?" she said.

She was wearing a new pink frilly housecoat with a low front and she hadn't too much on underneath. "What do you think?" I whispered into her ear. Knowing her weakness I thought it best to get steaming in at the start, so I put my arms round her and start kissing her quietly, putting the tension on when I feel the current's got going inside her.

Did I say *early* thirties? Well, on much closer inspection up and down I think I'd put her in her *late* thirties. She could be thirty-seven or thirty-eight, in fact she could be forty, topweight. But she's in beautiful condition. And when I say beautiful condition I don't mean she's in *hard* condition, like you get a good little working pony, but in perfect *soft* condition, like you get a filly that's been out to grass, not overworked, and is sleek, fat, round and has got a lovely glossy coat and is in good nick and rearing to go.

"Don't kiss me on the ear," she said, in a funny throaty voice, "you know what it does to me." One minute she's a big woman keeping me waiting at the door and the next she melts like a child in my arms. I mean at times she's like a child with a lollipop – she's no sooner coming to the end of one than she has one eye open for the next. No man – if he's human – can accommodate that. Well, up to a point I can. But only up to a point.

"I can handle it," I said.

"Give yourself time to take your jacket off," she said.

"I don't need to get my jacket off," I said.

I was just breaking free in a crafty way to get my breath and my bearings when she got hold of me and gave me one of her long passionate kisses. I won't go into detail, except to say that the feeling it left me with was almost exactly the same as I used to get when I was on the Preston run with a big lorry one time, and my landlady up there, Mrs. Bickerstaffe, used to give me a great feed of cowheel pie for dinner. You get a feeling of being full up right to the tonsils.

"I think I'll have a drink first," I said, when I did get my breath.

She went straight to the cocktail cabinet. I will say this for Ruby she's not a dawdler. She knows what she wants and if there's any going she's going to get it.

"What will you have?" she said in her best cut-glass voice.

I could see she wanted to get the formalities over and get down to business. I felt a large tumbler of egg flip wouldn't have been out of place. "I think I'll have a whisky," I said. "A Dimple Haig, if you've got it." I knew she hadn't. And to be quite frank I wouldn't know Dimple Haig from Long Tom except for the shape of the bottle, but I find I like reeling off a name now and again.

"I've got no Dimple," she said, "but I've got a Grant's."

"A Grant's Standfast?" I said, "That'll do nicely." I know it's a lot of play-acting but I get a kick out of throwing these little names about.

She poured me out what she must have thought was a generous whisky, but I find they never give me quite enough. But to be honest I've never met a woman yet who could be said to be liberal with the old whisky. I had a taste of it and it struck me that whisky wasn't what I wanted just then. I had this cowheel pie taste. It must have been her tongue or something.

"Here, you ain't got a beer have you?" I said, "a light ale or something – I'd fancy a chaser." A Scotch word that, chaser, very seldom you hear it down here.

"I've got some canned Pilsner in the fridge," she said.

"That's a gal," I said as she went into the little kitchen. Having got her hooked I felt I could play my cards easy. I looked round the flat – all off business expenses, I'll bet, and yet the working man has to pay his own bus fare. She came in pouring the beer into a long glass. She just didn't want to waste any time.

"Good health," I said.

"Cheers," she said, lifting her glass of brandy and ginger ale.

Here, that brandy reminds me of a funny thing about women in general, but more about Ruby, and I may as well get it out now whilst it's on my mind. The first time I took her out I says to her: "What you having?" So she says,

"A brandy and ginger ale. A Hennessey if they've got it." That's going to set me back a bit, I thought. Still I'll do anything once. So I go up to the bar and come back with a brandy and ginger ale and a light ale for myself. Now when we'd drunk up, I wait a minute to see if she's going to dip into her bag and at least *offer* to pay. But she don't. So I says to her: "What you having?" and she says: "Same again – a brandy and ginger ale." She's coming it a bit strong, I thinks – so I more or less cock a deaf 'un, and I go up to the bar and this time I come back with two light ales. I put one in front of her and one in front of me. So she stares at them and she looks at me and she says: "What's that?" and I says: "A light ale." And she says: "But I'm a *brandy* drinker." So I says to her: "That might be, but I ain't a brandy *buyer*. If you want a brandy and ginger ale, you go and get yourself one."

Now it was touch and go for a minute, if you see what I mean. But then she saw where she stood. The light must have dawned on her. She drank her light ale and we got on beautifully. In fact she got her hand into her bag and paid the next round – and had her brandy and ginger ale, to which she was entitled. In fact, I had one too to keep her company. With women like that you've got to know your own mind. And I've always said that most women don't mind paying, what a woman doesn't like is being under obligation. They start growing resentful under it.

"Know what, Ruby," I said, after I'd had a drink of this ice-cold Pilsner, "I think them fridges take the taste out of everything. Things taste more of *cold* than they do of what they should taste of."

A mate of mine bought his wife a fridge and he reckons his stomach hasn't been right since. He wants a drink of milk and he takes a sup from the bottle out of the fridge and it chills his stomach. Matter of fact, I do believe anything too cold paralyses your taste buds, if you see what I mean. I reckon you can't beat the old fashioned box larder with perforated zinc round for keeping things at the right temperature. Ruby wasn't going to be drawn.

"Ruby," I said, "a small favour –"

"What's that?" she said.

"Will you not stick your nails into me like you did last Wednesday? You left bloody great long scratches all down my back."

She laughed: "It was worth it, wasn't it?" she said.

It was for you, I thought. Great long weals they were – dug her nails right in she did. I took another drink of the whisky and chased it down with the lager.

"I thought I'd put my brand on you," she said. "Keep the others off."

"What others?" I said.

"The others," she said.

Somebody's been talking to her, I thought. It must be that time I took her to the club and Sharpey and Perce were there.

She's had these two husbands. Both dead. And as I gave my back a rub it struck me that I had a bleeding good idea what they must have died of. She don't spare you.

"Don't put your cold glass on my polished table," she said. She thinks more of her polished table than she do of my poor back, I thought. Still it had almost been worth it – at the time. Nearly everything is worth it at the time. I suppose they've got to have their bit of pleasure as well.

"Don't be so fussy," I said. I play up to them a bit and then I find I'm off going my own way. I chanced to knock a rose out of a big bowl she had on this table and she put it back and began to arrange them. She looked at me and said: "Do you ever think of taking flowers to your lady friends, Alfie?"

"I often think about it," I said, "but I never do it. Not unless they're in hospital."

When I said that the memory suddenly came back to me about the bunch of freesias I'd taken to little Gilda that time she'd gone into hospital to have Malcolm. A thought will often drop in on me like that, a little moment from the past, you could say, and for a second the inside of me lights up with these faces that have gone. Know what – it makes you feel like a bleeding old man. I mean I could even see his face – his two faces come to that, what he was as an infant and what he was when they took him away from me. I came over choked at the thought. Because that's something they can never make up again to you – a child's only a child once. And there in front of me is this big lustbox Ruby, and I felt like picking up this big bowl of roses and flinging them through the bloody window and straight down onto the pavement outside. I mean just for a minute that ponced-up flat made me feel sick. Of course I controlled myself. You've got to do.

"What's up, Alfie?" she said.

"Nothing," I said.

I got up and went to her bathroom. I must admit she had a smashing bath, put in special, primrose yellow, with all these mirrors round no matter which way you looked. Agreed it got a bit tight-fitting with the two of us in, she was some size was Ruby, but I'd had lots of fun splashing about and whatnot. The tricks we'd got up to in that bath. Yes, there were times when I'd felt lucky to step out of it alive. This Gilda had definitely misguided me. She'd made out she couldn't live without me – but she could. It's not playing the game really.

"I'm not fussy, am I?" said Ruby, coming in the bathroom behind me, and putting her arms round me. What can you do?

"You are fussy," I said.

"I'm not fussy," she said and she put her arms round the back of my neck and started kissing me and pressing her middle against me.

"You're a proper little sex pot, ain't you," I said.

"Yes," she said, "I'm a sex pot but I'm not fussy. Am I, Alfie?"

Know what, she seemed to have a tender look or something in her eye. As though I'd hurt her. She's mumsie inside as well as outside, I thought, if she'd only give way to it. "Course you're not," I said and I kissed her. I quite like the smell of a bathroom – I mean all the mixed smells hanging about. And you can't be seen. I started slipping off her housecoat. After all, life has to go on. And same as I say, she's in such beautiful condition.

CHAPTER TWENTY

I'D done a couple of weddings one Saturday morning and I'm through about two o'clock. So I go into the pub and start pinting it with Sharpey and Perce. I had a feeling not to go in the first place – it came over me as I'm going in the door – because I've told Annie I'd be back for lunch. I'd never been one for eating much in the middle of the day, or if I did then I wouldn't want much at night, but somehow she's got me into the habit of eating at both times. Know what, I've come round to thinking that if there's one thing worse than never having a meal put in front of you, it's keep having food put in front of you all day long. She was a one for her cups of tea and bits of cake. They seem to have a notion up North that if you ain't eating every five minutes you'll drop dead. Course, I must admit I'd never been as well looked after in all my life as with that little bird in the home. And it's one thing to eat little when you've only got little to eat and it's quite another to eat little when you've got a lot.

Anyway, I'm bevying away with these two, and Perce is telling us about a driver called Little Benny. Now it seems this Benny is off on his night run up to Liverpool, and whilst he's having a cup of tea in a caff at Barnet he gets his wagon and load knocked off. So he telephones for the police. Of course, the police naturally think he's in on the job. Oddly enough he ain't. So it's well past midnight when they let him go. He gets a lift back to Peckham, and when he creeps in home so's not to disturb his wife, he only finds her in bed with his shunter. In case you don't know, that's the bloke who's handed him the wagon and papers over at the depot.

"What did Benny do?" said Sharpey.

"What can he do?" said Perce. "This geezer's twice his size, and Benny's missis must be all of twelve stone."

"I'd have smashed their bleedin' heads in with a hammer," said Sharpey.

"Now what good would that have done – a couple of

dead bodies on his hands? He'd have ruined the bedclothes into the bargain," said Perce. "Anyway, he's got these five kids and they've got to be looked after."

"What did he do?" I said. It's a funny situation. He wouldn't have minded her having it off so much – although it's not a nice thing with five kids in the next room, and the bloke your shunter, so that the chat is sure to spread – but what is definitely wrong is for her to let him catch her at it. It don't give a geezer any proper way out.

"Benny said that when this bloke gets out of bed," said Perce, "he gets in beside her. He didn't fancy it all that much, one on top of the other, you could say, but same as he said, when you come to weigh it up, what else could he do?"

"He was in what you call a dilemma," I said, "and in one of them it's often best to take the simplest way out."

"I tell you I'd have smashed their bleedin' heads in with a hammer," said Sharpey. "That would have been the simplest way for me."

"Then you do it," I said.

"It's time," said Vi, the barmaid, "it's nearly three."

"Same again," said Sharpey, "three pints."

"Just top my pint up with a light ale, Vi," I said. I didn't want another pint, in fact I didn't want any more ale at all.

Perce turned to me. "You got your car outside, Alfie? You could run us round to the club."

Suddenly I became aware of this little man that comes onto my shoulder at times. He likes whispering into my ear. I suppose everybody's got one. *She'll have your dinner all ready now, Alfie,* he whispered, *and she'll be waiting for you – you'd better get going.*

"I don't think I'll bother going round to the club," I said. *She'll have a nice clean pinny to greet you with,* he said.

"You'll enjoy an hour or two at the club," said Sharpey, "it'll make a change."

"I don't think I'll bother," I said.

After all, why run them round to the club, I thought, I'm not their hired chauffeur. At the same time this little man had another rabbit: *When you go indoors, Alfie,* he said, *she'll have everything clean and spotless, and as soon as you take your things off, she'll start washing them. As soon as you wipe your nose, she'll take that hanky out of your pocket and boil it. And you'll no sooner have your socks off than she'll be kneading and squeezing them in Surf.*

"What's come over you lately, Alfie?" said Perce.

"Come over me?" I said, "nothing. Why? Good health."

"Well, why don't you come round?" said Sharpey.

There was something telling me not to tell them – not this little man, something else. I've usually got one or two little voices going on in my head. I don't think it's that I'm a nutter or anything of that sort, I think it's just that I'm open minded. I thought, I'll just let them see how well off I am compared with them.

"I've got this little kid called Annie staying at my gaff," I said. "She's from the North and she can't half cook."

"What's cooking got to do with it?" said Perce.

"She don't like it if he ain't home for his meals on time," said Vi. "That so, Alfie?"

This Vi ain't a bad-looker, and she can never make it out why I don't play up to her like most of the other blokes do. Now the reason for that is this: I used to have it off with a woman who served in a transport caff – in fact I've had it off with more than one in that line – and right enough she was good for the odd packet of cigarettes, cup of tea, bacon sandwich, and so on, was this woman, but somehow she always seemed to be hovering about near me so that I never felt free. It ain't worth it for your freedom of mind – the odd sandwich or cup of tea. I've tried it as well with one or two landladies, and sometimes with their daughters, but somehow it don't never work out satisfactorily in the long run. It seems they get familiar or something. You've given it to them once so they begin to take it for granted. I don't like anything like that. I like to keep my place so let them keep theirs. Now by playing it dead cool with Vi I've found I get far better service, and after all that's what you go to a pub for. Not to chat up some soppy blonde behind the counter. The blokes who fuss round her get no thanks.

"She doesn't mind what time I get home," I said, "and she makes some real 'andsome nosh-ups she do."

"Vi," said Perce, taking a last swig at his pint, "giss three more quick pints."

"Too late," she said.

"Not for me," I said.

"Not like you, Alfie," said Vi, "heel tapping."

"Draw us two quick pints, Vi," said Perce.

Vi starts drawing them.

"What was you saying about this little bird?" said Sharpey.

"I was just saying she makes a marvellous steak-and-kidney pie," I said.

"I hate the taste of kidneys," said Perce. "They've got a sort of dead flavour about 'em."

"Offal," said Sharpey. He looked at me. "I thought you was looking a bit blown out. What do you say, Vi?"

"What do you mean *blown out*?" I said, and I give myself a thump in the stomach. To be quite frank, I was feeling a bit duff in the guts, but I wasn't going to let them see it. I mean you can't be well fed without filling up.

"I was only saying you looked blown out. Don't you think so, Vi?" said Sharpey.

"He's certainly put some fat on," said Vi, and she began to look me up and down.

"Fat! *me!*" I said. "What are you talking about – fat?"

"Don't take offence, Alfie," said Perce, "it's just the appearance."

"What appearance?" I said.

Now Sharpey and Perce looked me up and down from tip to toe and then turned away and said nothing. Then I can hear this little man break in again: *You know what, Alfie, that little gaff ain't your'n any more, it's her'n.* Come to think of it he wasn't far out. It meant more to her than it did to me, and I suppose that's *one* way of something belonging to you.

"Here's the *two* pints," said Vi, putting them on the counter.

"Make it three," I said, putting down a quid. "It's my turn anyway." I had to force my beer down, and there was nothing said for a minute or two, only you could feel some thinking was going on, then Perce turned to me, looking very sympathetic and said: "It don't really suit you, you know, Alfie."

"What don't suit me?" I said.

"This *poncified* look you got," he said.

"What *poncified* look?" I said.

"You look all puffed out," said Sharpey, and he tried to get hold of my cheeks with his fingers.

"Turn it in," I said, "and stop mouthing about it. I tell you I've never felt fitter in all my life." I picked up the new pint and downed half of it at one go. My guts were feeling all swelled out. "It's the way she keeps feeding you, Alfie," said this little man, "she's getting you all fattened out."

"Don't misunderstand him – he wasn't saying you wasn't fit, was you, Sharpey?" said Perce. "All he was saying was what with your collar looking so tight on you, and your trousers like they are, and that jacket gripping you tight under the armpits you were looking a bit –"

"Poncified," said Sharpey, "in other words blown out."

"That's it," said Perce, "blown out sort of."

I turned to him. "Are you going to go on making a mouth of it, Sharpey?" I said.

"Now don't get excited," said Perce.

"Know what, Alfie?" said Sharpey, "I reckon that Annie of your'n must be putting the block on you and you can't see it. What do you say, Perce?"

"The kid's only looking after me," I said.

"Don't be a nit," said Perce, "that's the way every bint puts the block on a bloke, by looking after him. Getting him dependent, see. Isn't that so, Vi?"

"It's one of the ways," said Vi.

"In twelve months' time you won't recognise yourself," said Sharpey, "you'll be stuffed to the ears with all that bleedin' hot-pot."

"I tell you she's only looking after me," I said.

"She's softening you up, mate, ready for the kill," said Perce.

They're jealous that's what they are, I kept telling myself. What man isn't who can see a mate being better looked after by a bird than he is. Men detest that sort of thing, they all want to be in the same boat. If there's one thing a drunk can't stand is seeing somebody else sober. But at the time I couldn't see all these things because I've got this little man as well to contend with. I don't know whether we've each got what they call an evil thing in us – I shouldn't be at all surprised – that whispers and tells us things that go against our better understanding. But same as I say, I definitely do hear this little man and other things, and the funny thing is this – if I don't do what he tells me it nearly always turns out wrong. It might come right for the start but it'll be wrong for the finish. *If you have her around much longer, Alfie* he kept saying, *she'll change you that much that you won't be able to recognise yourself.* He must have known that the one thing I detest is the idea of having a woman change me.

"I'll run you round to the club after all," I said.

"That's my boy," said Sharpey, "good old Alfie."

"I knew you'd see the light," said Perce.

Vi kept on wiping the glasses and looking at me.

CHAPTER TWENTY-ONE

I COULD never understand Sharpey and Perce that day. I don't know how it was I didn't tumble they were needling me, but there was something else behind it. They came out with a very funny stroke in that club. They're standing side by side, and you can see there's something going on between them, and Sharpey said to me: "Are you still doing a line with that big bird, Alfie?"

"What big bird?" I said.

"The hairdresser bint," said Perce. "The one you once brought round here."

"She ain't a hairdresser," I said, "anyway who told you?"

"It owns some hairdresser's shops," said Sharpey, "and it lives in that big block across the river."

"Well, what about it?" I said.

"Well, you want to look out," said Sharpey, "a mate of your'n is after it."

"What mate?" I said.

"Never mind what mate. You want to keep an eye on it. What d'you say, Perce?"

"Say nothing," said Perce. "He's after you as well Alfie."

I couldn't make out head or tail what they were talking

about and they wouldn't tell me any more, but I could see there was *something* behind it. Who could be after me?

Anyway, I dropped them off and then went round to my own gaff. I wasn't drunk. Somehow their chat had sobered me, but sobered me nasty, if you see what I mean. On top of it I'd had this little man on my shoulder. Ain't it funny how when life seems to be going on beautiful it can suddenly turn rotten on you. Then I'd gone on gin-and-tonics in the club and I find them sobering up after beer. In fact, the more I drank the more dead sober I went. Gin does that up to a point. I started thinking how it used to be before I met Annie, how I could go out with a free mind, all my troubles under my hat, as they say, and drink and do what I wanted without ever a thought of someone waiting for me. I find I don't care for that feeling of having somebody waiting for me at home. It's like you're plagued with something behind your mind all the time. I know some blokes who love the feeling, but I do like leaving a room empty and feeling it'll still be empty when I get back. Well it's nice to get away from human beings now and again. And another funny thing is this – it's a bigger burden for you to have some nice bird waiting for you than a real bitchy piece – because you won't mind how long you keep a bitch waiting, if you follow me.

I was definitely getting fatter. That was a certainty. I'd never been used to regular meals and I think I felt more myself when I didn't have them. All any man needs is one good meal a day. He don't want a woman keep shoving cups of tea and bits of cake on him. Course they only do that because they want some themselves. The idea behind *Feed the brute* is that you can be feeding yourself at the same time. A man can go on nearly all day without ever thinking of food, but food, cooking, shopping, never seem to be out of a woman's mind. Know what, a man's wits are not nearly as sharp if he's being well fed. I'll bet if you put two rats in a cage, one well fed and the other kept hungry, that hungry one will run rings round the other. It's the same with the other – if you're getting it regular you seem to come over half blind, and many a nice piece of crumpet will escape you, just for the want of you taking notice. I'm always working things like that out in my little mind and I always end up with the same question: what's the bleeding answer?

I could smell old Annie's cooking along the landing before I came to the door. She came out of the kitchen as I went in. "Is that you, Alfie?" she said.

What a question to ask, I thought, I'm only standing in front of her. "Yeh, it's me. I'm only about five hours late, ain't I. Start rucking me." I half wished in my mind that she'd have had that rotten song on the record-player about the geezer who's supposed to want the bird when she no longer wants him. I'd have smashed the thing up if she had, but she hadn't.

"Your dinner's ready," she said. She didn't look the least put out. In a way I wish she had. She looked surprised that I should expect her to be peeved. They've got you every way. She went to the top of the oven and brought out something in a pie dish with a crust on the top. I looked at it. "You ain't made another bleedin' hotpot!" I said.

"Oh no –" she said. "It's a steak and kidney pie."

"It's the same thing, ain't it," I said.

"Not at all," she said. "There's all the difference in the world between a hotpot and a steak-and-kidney pie."

"Well, don't bother to tell me," I said.

She picked up a knife and she cut a slice out of this thick brown crust on the top, and all this juicy meaty smell came out as the steam came off it. It's the sort of thing that smells good if you're hungry, but don't mean a thing if you ain't. I pointed my finger into the pie, where I could see all these pieces of meat in this brown juicy gravy. "It's the same as all them North Country dishes," I said. "It's a bleedin' blower-out."

I could see she didn't know which way to turn. She had no definite pointer about whether she should start serving it or put it away. I expect she thought that given a bit of time she could ride it. "Why can't we have something out of a can for a change?" I said. "I used to get some lovely meals out of cans. Spam, Libby's corned beef, baked beans and pork, John West's Salmon, sardines – handsome grub all that was. I mean you don't taste those meals until you begin to eat them, but these hot dishes you can already taste coming along the landing. You feel you've had enough when you sit down. They overface a bloke."

"But you always said you like my steak-and-kidney pie, Alfie," she said.

"Listen," I said, to her, "if I get that lot on top of a skinful of ale I'll hardly be able to draw my breath. I'll get a horrible feeling of being full up, blown out – poncified." And to suit my words a great long burping rift of wind came out of me that would have blown up a set of bagpipes.

She looked at me, and she looked at the pie on the table, and she shook out the little kitchen cloth she's brought it in with her, and she turns her head on one side and she says, "You used to say once that you loved that feeling of being really full up. You said you'd never had it in all your life until you met me." They're always quick to remind you of what you didn't have before you met them. It never seems to strike them that in the long run what a bloke didn't have might suit him far better than what he did have.

"What I loved once," I said, "and what I love now are two different things."

"Have you been out with that man Sharpey?" she said.

"What about it if I have?" I said.

"He's no friend of yours," she said.

"I'll decide who're my friends and who ain't," I said, and began to strip off my clothes. "Where's my American shirt?"

"Are you going out again, Alfie?" she said.

"I asked you where my American shirt was," I said.

"The blue one?" she said, "– it's in the drawer."

"Nah, not the blue, the pink."

"Oh I washed it whilst you were out," she said. "It'll soon be dry. I could iron it then."

"What did you have to wash it for?" I said, "I only wore it a couple of hours."

"I thought it would feel fresher for you," she said.

The idea behind my mind was that she might have thought that any shirt needed washing after I'd worn it for a couple of hours. I didn't say it because I had a feeling it might be true. I don't just mean that she might think it needed washing – but that it did need washing. I mean you let any sensitive bloke smell his own dried-out sweaty shirt and he's in for a shock.

"Know what Annie," I said, "I do believe you only wash to fill in your bleedin' time."

"Why should I?" she said.

"So that you won't have a spare empty minute on your hands," I said. "You've got to keep yourself on the go." Her face came over guilty – I spotted it.

"Why should I keep on the go?" she said.

"To get *him* out of your mind," I said.

"To get who out of my mind?" she said. She looked upset. She's very pale all of a sudden. I could feel this little man egging me on. Of course I'm not making excuses for myself. You've got to do what you have to do. I went up to her. "That bloody Tony, or whatever you call him," I said, "what you've been writing about in your little diary."

"Have you been reading my diary?" she said.

"You say you can't get him out of your mind," I said, "no matter how much you try. '*Tony was on my mind all day long*'."

"Alfie," she said, "have you been in my bag and read my diary?" She's only trying to make out it's a crime. I mean the first thing you do with any bird is go through its handbag – if you get the chance. I mean that can tell you a lot more than a face can. It's an eye-opener sometimes.

"And why shouldn't I?" I said.

"You shouldn't," she said. "Those are my secret thoughts."

"You're not entitled to any secret thoughts," I said, "if you're living with me." I knew I was wrong when I said it. Not that that's ever stopped me from saying a thing. I mean if you ain't entitled to your thoughts, and all thoughts are a secret in some way, then you're entitled to nothing. On the other hand, you don't want a bird around that keeps harbouring thoughts, if you see what I mean.

"You can't help having thoughts," she said.

"No, but you can help writing the bleedin' things down and lettin' me see 'em," I said.

She seemed to see the logic of that.

125

"I only wrote them down," she said, "to get them out of me."

What does she want to think about a bloke called Tony for when I'm around? It's like there's three people living in the one room, sharing the one bed, come to that, and one of 'em you can't see and you can't get hold of. I mean nobody has any right to inflict somebody they happen to love on somebody else they happen to be living with. I mean if I'm in bed with one bird, and I'm thinking of another, it means in fact I'm having neither of 'em, if you see what I mean. Of course I could be wrong. Though it's not often I am.

Well there's Annie standing so innocent beside the table, rabbiting away about her secret thoughts, and there's me and I can't do a thing about them. Don't think I was jealous – I wasn't. I've trained myself too well – I never think about things I can't do anything about. Well, very seldom. So on the impulse of the moment I grab hold of her steak-and-kidney pie from where it's standing on the table – and nearly burned my hands into the bargain, though I didn't notice it at the time – and I said to her:

"Well I'll just show you what I think about you – your secret thoughts and your effin' steak-and-kidney pie!" And with that I flung that dish as hard as I could against the wall.

To be quite frank, I shocked myself when I saw what I'd let myself do. I don't mean when I threw it, I mean when it hit the wall. It was a clean shot – it could hardly be anything else at that range – and the crust and the rim of the dish made a solid hit. It wasn't as loud as you might expect, but it made a horrible thud. Then it let out a loud, ugly sucking noise, and some of the dish dropped in pieces, and the gravy splashed a bit, but mainly it all began to crawl in a thick brown stream down the wall.

Annie looked at it quite calmly. I'd given her one shock, so that might have put her beyond reach of another. She looked at me then. Know what – there was no hate in it. It was just a look, if you see what I mean. I'll tell you what I felt like. I felt like it served her bleeding right. Just as easy, I suppose, I could have felt like leaning against her breast and saying how sorry I was and what a rotten horrible mean thing it was, and what a shit I was, and would she forgive me.

I said nothing and did nothing, but just stood there. She moved first. She walked very quietly across to the bed, and bent down and felt underneath, and brought out her little suitcase. Then she went to the drawer that I'd allowed her in the chest of drawers and began to take out her bits of things. It didn't take her long, not more than a minute or two to collect all her belongings.

"Don't take nothing that don't belong to you," I said, when I saw what she was about. She didn't say anything to that – she just got her little raincoat off of the nail behind the door and put it over her arm and picked up her suitcase. She did it all so quiet like, as if in the end she had expected nothing better. Or it may have been the explosion of the pie dish that made it all sound so quiet after. Just then, as she was going out of the door, she turned and said to me in this funny flat North Country voice she's got: "Don't let your custard spoil – it's in the oven." Then she closed the door very gently behind her and went off.

For a second or two I stood there a bit dazed. I hadn't expected she'd go off. What a stroke to come out with though: "*Don't let your custard spoil.*" I went and opened the oven door.

Sure enough there was something inside. I've put my hands in to take it out, see, but the dish is hot, so I pick up a cloth and I take it out with that. I could hardly believe my eyes. It was the handsomest custard you ever saw. It was a lovely golden egg brown, with a nice little nutmeggy smell. For a second I felt choked, I did straight. I thought: whilst you've been thinking bad of her, Alfie, she's been thinking good of you. It gives you a shock, see, when you've been putting the poison in for somebody in your mind, and you find out they've been putting the honey in for you.

I walked to the table with the custard, whispering to myself, *Annie, Annie, Annie.* It suddenly seemed like it was a lovely name. Looking down on that custard it seemed as if I could see in it all the kind and thoughtful little things she'd done for me. All the shirts, socks and other things she'd

127

washed for me, all the little buttons she'd sewed on my clothes without me having to tell her, all the times when I'd come home and found she'd cleaned all my shoes for me, and the marvellous way she had of ironing my hankies, and the way she'd once undressed me and put me to bed and cleaned up all my clobber when I'd come home drunk one time. All these little thoughts got together and flooded my mind. I never go after anybody, but I ran to the door, and raced down the stairs after her, calling out "*Annie!*"

It's funny how soon somebody you know can disappear in a street. You go to the corner and look and there seems about half a dozen ways they could have gone. And there's buses and that going by, and you think how they might easily be on one of them. And you begin to stare at people, thinking some old woman might be the one you're looking for.

There wasn't a sight of little Annie anywhere.

Know what? – I was that choked when I went back and saw her custard on the table that it was a good ten minutes before I could get down to scoffing it!

BOOK THREE

"If you haven't got peace of mind you've got nothing"

CHAPTER TWENTY-TWO

IT's turned eleven one Sunday morning and I can hear the old church bells ringing, and there I am, bringing up an extra shine to my black shoes with the corner of a blanket hanging off of the bed. I look round my little gaff and I've got to admit it looks a right dump since little Annie went. But I do feel at home in it, and I don't care what anybody says, that's the main thing. I mean all I ask of the pad I live in is that I know where everything is; that there's room round the walls to hang up my suits and that it don't have too many funny smells. Even though my place now looks so untidy, I know where things are, but when Annie was here I had to keep asking her where everything was. She kept moving things round and taking my clothes off of chairs and putting them in drawers.

Know what, I think sausages taste best if you eat 'em straight out the frying-pan. You seem to lose the flavour once you keep moving food from one thing to another. Besides that, I like eating as I'm cooking – it's more healthy. And it gives you a chance to chew your food longer – standing up.

Mind you, I will admit I could have missed her around the place for the first few days, especially when I came home of an evening and opened the door, and instead of a nice warm shining room with the smell of cooking there would be this cold stale room with lots of dirty dishes on the table. But same as I used to tell myself – in twenty minutes, mate, you won't know the difference. Nor did I. The fact is, I'm not really cut out for that sort of life with a woman. The next thing they expect you to start passing the salt or sugar or something, instead of reaching out for it themselves. I hate anything like that. When I'm down to my grub I like to keep my eye on my own plate and forget everybody else.

On top of this, they start asking you questions: "What would you like for your evening meal?" Now who wants to think about what he'll want to eat in a few hours' time. Then they say: "Will you have your eggs boiled or fried?" All things like that, making a simple life complicated, where you have to think. She was even asking, "What time will you be back?" Now that is one thing that do get on my wick.

Leave all that stuff out. I'll tell you the real trouble. I've had time to think it over these weeks: Annie was turning my little gaff into a *home*. I mean a home for herself as well as for me. Now a home's a very funny set-up. A very funny set-up indeed. It's really a place for people who've got some kind of a private *need* for each other, if you follow me. I ain't got a *need* for nobody. My home is *outside* four walls – not inside. So in fact Annie was infringing on my liberty, if you see what I mean.

So there you are. She can be the best little bint in the world but if she infringes on your liberty, I mean of mind as well as of body, it just ain't worth it. Leastways that's how I look at it, because once a bird has taken your liberty away, she's taken *you* away. You might as well be a bloody performing dog because you're doing what she wants and not what you want, and I'd sooner be what I am, a mongrel roaming around the streets, if you see what I mean.

Know what, I was chatting Perce one day, telling him how I'd slung little Annie out, but not giving him the real details – I mean, he wouldn't cotton on to the real thing no matter what I told him – when he came across with a stroke that shook me. "Here, I'll tell you something," said Perce, "did you know that Sharpey kept trying to pull Annie when you were out?" I said it wouldn't surprise me. "Them Sundays you went out," he said, "he used to call round on some pretext or other and try to lap it up, but it seems Annie wouldn't wear him. He kept making out to her what a dead villain you was. But she just didn't want to know. She even kept the door locked against him." Then it struck me that must have been why he put the poison in for her in the pub.

Mind you, I never mentioned it to Sharpey. What good could it do. Forgive and forget. And after all, thinking it over, I didn't want her back.

I mean she was too good for me, little Annie, toiling away like she did made me feel uncomfortable at times. So that in the end it was a relief to get rid of her. I mean, when you get down to it, the average man must know in his own heart what a rotten bleeder he is, he don't want someone good around to keep reminding him of it. That's why a good bloke will always prefer to marry a real bitch. It means he's doing his purgatory on earth. Every time she does the dirty on him he's got another reason for looking up to Heaven.

I've started tidying up the place because I'm expecting a visitor. But you'd never guess who it's going to be. At least I don't think you would. There's a quiet little knock on the door and I go and open it. She's standing there in her blue C. & A. coat, with her handbag, a little B.O.A.C. bag and her basket.

"Come in, Lily," I said to her. She walked into the room very shyly, trying not to look round. You can see she's never been in a gaff like this in her life. "You're a bit early, gal," I said.

"I didn't want to be late," she said, "I caught an early train. Is he coming?"

Lily love – you look nothing, but you know what – I could bleeding cry for you and your sort. Talk about warriors – talk about soldiers, give me a little Mum with three kids and living respectable if a bit in debt and she'll put them all to shame for bleeding guts. I find I've got to watch myself lately, I get these funny strokes of feeling coming over me.

"He said he'd be here about twelve o'clock," I said. "Why don't you take your coat off. Make yourself at home."

I helped her off with her coat. Her hands felt very cold. "Are you worried?" I said to her.

"A bit," she said, "but it'll be all right."

Here, talking about some wives and their husbands and families, there's a bloke I know called Tim Townsend, a transport boss, married and has a family of five, all growing up, when his wife has to go in hospital with a cancer. Of course she's left it too late. She ain't been thinking of herself. Now it's the day before she dies, see, and he's driven round about two o'clock to have a chat with her. "Tim," she says, "you haven't had your lunch, have you, I can tell it by your cheekbones. Now you see you get some or you'll worry me." He told me she had a long rabbit about him and his lunch as though she had nothing else on her mind, and that the day before she kicked the bucket. Now do you see what I mean?

"You look all dark under the eyes," I said.

"I didn't sleep so well last night," she said.

I'll bet you never had a wink, I thought.

"There's nothing to worry about," I said. "He's a proper skilled man, works at a hospital or something. They reckon there's nothing to it. It's like having a tooth out, only it don't hurt. Here, what have you got in the basket?"

"I had to make an excuse," she said, "so I said I was visiting Harry as usual. I hope nobody finds out."

"People only know what you tell 'em," I said. Quite false, but I thought it would serve for there and then.

"I've written and told him I have a cold and it seems better not to go in case I give it to him," she said.

It brought old Harry back to mind when I saw the jar of home-made marmalade, the calves' foot jelly and the biscuits. Come to think of it, there was some kind of peace in my system in those days in the san.

"Will you get rid of them for me?" she said.

"I'll use 'em up one way or another," I said. I began to take the things out of her basket. Down at the bottom I saw an envelope sticking out. "There's a letter here."

"It's from young Phil to Harry," she said.

I looked and saw the squiggley writing on the outside. I didn't know what to say. She put it into her handbag.

"Is there a – ?" she said.

"You mean a toilet?" I said. "Sure, it's on the landing. Here, I'll show you. Come on." I took her out to the W.C. on the landing. I was glad I'd given it a cleaning that morning. Then I went back into the room.

CHAPTER TWENTY-THREE

Just fancy, Lily, old Harry's wife! And it was funny how I'd got myself involved there. I'd gone out to the sanatorium one Sunday, see, just to let them have a proper look at me. I mean they'd only seen me in captivity, they hadn't seen how I looked when I was really dressed up; and somehow I'd got that bit attached to them all. Here, a funny thing happened. There's this little Gina, see, what I was so intimate with. Know what, when she saw me all dressed up she didn't want to know. I mean, you could have understood it if it had been the other way about – I had been dependent on her and I no longer was. But now it's Gina who don't want to know, so that's another of those little things turn out quite the opposite to what you expect.

Now I've had a nice hour or so – except for this cool interlude with Gina – and I'm just going off when old Harry asks me am I going Maidenhead way back, so that I can give Lily a lift in my car. As a matter of fact I'm not, I'm going back by Wokingham and Ascot. But just to please him I say I could go back that way.

Now it's one of the worst mistakes you can make – going out of your way to oblige somebody. It's very rare I do it, but whenever I do you can bet something is sure to go wrong. I'm not cut out for that boy scout lark, because if ever I do a good deed it always seems to rebound on me. The funny thing is, Lily doesn't want to come in the car either. I can tell it by the look on her face. So we both agree just to oblige old Harry, lying there in bed. Never oblige a sick person – no good comes of it.

Lily sits there in silence as I'm driving along, and seeing how ribby she looks and thinking how it would be a nice thing for old Harry's sake, I drive a roundabout way by the river, and on top of that I ask her would she like some tea. The thought had never struck her and she doesn't know what to say. Now I've got old Ruby's Zodiac with me, automatic drive, Windsor Grey, real leather individual seats.

That's a car you can take anywhere. So's I've seen one of these big hotels and I've driven straight in. It's a place with these green lawns running right down to the side of the river and little tables set out by themselves under the trees. I quite like anything like that at times. Mind you, you're paying for the view as well as for your tea. All the little cafes about were crowded but this place is nearly empty, except for a few toffs and I see the reason why when I look at the price. It's eight-and-six for tea, whilst the other places are only four shillings. Anyway, I lead Lily across to a nice little table by itself just near the edge of the water. She's nervous, and I can see she's never been in a place like this before. Now the waiter comes up, an old boy he is, and he gives me a look as much as to say, I know what you are. So I looks back at him as much as to say, and I know what you are. And you know what you can go and do with yourself. Nothing said, see, just dodgy looks. So he starts trying to stare me out but I stare holes in him I do. "We only serve the set tea," he says. "Yes," I says, "a set tea for madam and I."

That old geezer is going to spoil the tea for me, I think. Funny, how they can knock you off your perch. Anyway, he comes back nice and steady with the tea, and I can see he's had a change of heart, so I cools down. "Let me know if you need more hot water, sir," he says. Know what, I slipped him a couple of bob there and then. I know it's manners to wait till you're leaving but why delay a good impulse. It was the "Sir".

Lily pours the tea and it comes out nice and strong, and what with these cucumber sandwiches, and fresh scones, whipped cream and blackcurrant jelly, I notice she's slowly coming to life. A woman can fade away if she don't get attention. I mean there are good things going in this life, but they never seem to get the way of women like that. She's feeding the ducks, see, and there's some little baby ducklings darting in and out around their mum, and as she's watching, Lily gets a nice little smile come to the corner of her mouth. There are women like that who look dead ordinary until they smile and then they kind of come up. I was quite touched by that little smile I was, and I thought to myself, she couldn't have been too bad a few years ago. Anyway, I feel quite set up after that tea, what with the waiter calling me Sir and Ruby's big Zodiac parked there in the drive. I was going to leave him another shilling but it don't do to overdo a good thing.

I thought I'd like to stretch my legs, the day being so nice. So I've taken Lily for a walk along the towpath. Well we come to a quiet little spot there by the Thames, nice and secluded it is, and we sit ourselves down on the warm grass and I'm talking about Harry and how he used to be on visiting days, always watching out for her and pretending he was reading, when the next thing she gives a gulp or something and I sees at once I've said the wrong thing. She's crying away, so I put my hand on her shoulder and try to comfort her. I could feel she was all of a shake underneath, and just because she's a woman and most women would expect to be kissed at a time like that, I've kissed her, ain't I.

It started out as a friendly peck on the side of her cheek, and it seemed to work its way around to a full kiss on the lips. Having lain in a bed next to her husband for months on end I couldn't do less than kiss her, out of my friendship for him, if you see what I mean. Now, whilst I'm still kissing her I can feel her sobs going quiet, and to my surprise I senses that nature or something has started working in her. It was the last thing I expected. Then I think to myself, *what harm can it do?* My trouble is – I've never learnt how to refuse something for nothing, even when I don't need it. But what man has?

It'll settle her little mind, I tell myself, and she must be badly in need of it. Harry will never know, and even if he did he's no right to begrudge me – or her come to that. It'll round off the tea nicely. After all, that tea had cost me nineteen shillings with the tip, not to mention the extra petrol going a long way round. It's funny how many things do go through a bloke's mind at a time like that. And at the same time I can feel this little man that sometimes comes on my shoulder, and he's trying to say, *Leave it alone, Alfie.* But I don't listen to him. What man does when he's told, leave it alone.

Now I don't know whether it was the fresh air, the whipped cream and jelly, the cucumber sandwiches or old Harry's missus never having had it off with a man in all that time, but the whole job was over and done with in about three minutes flat, give five seconds either way. Not that I'd rushed it. I'd thought about her. I bet that was more than old Harry ever had. I'm not that sort of peasant. But I hadn't dallied about too much, if you see what I mean.

"Know what Lily," I said, "I quite enjoyed that."

I had too. When a man has learnt to enjoy *that,* and knows he's enjoyed it, and admits he's enjoyed it, and feels thankful in his heart for having had it, then I say he's halfway to becoming a happy man. It seemed to have taken me out of myself, as they say, relaxed me handsome. You can't beat fresh air. "That was very nice, gal," I said, and I gave her an encouraging pat on the back. What I say is – if you enjoy a thing show a bit of appreciation.

Then I took out my best hanky and wiped the corner of her eyes, where there were stains of teardrops still showing. "My, but that's done you a world of good!" I said. It had too. It seemed in under five minutes she had come up quite lovely, her little face and everything, as she was lying there on the grass with the afternoon sun coming across the Thames from the West. What a marvellous tonic it can be – if people only knew it.

It must have been the first time in months that she'd let herself go. Just imagine, from early morning till late night keeping a tight hold of yourself. She starts off about seven every morning messing about and doing for her kids, scrubbing 'em, cooking for 'em, nagging 'em, and listening to 'em. Then, I expect she's worried about the bills and making ends meet, and if she's a spare minute she's got to sit down and write to Harry. I'll bet even in her sleep she must be worrying. Then comes this little off moment of pleasure from out of the blue, when she can forget all that, and all her little body's instincts can't believe it and come rushing out to have their twopenn'orth. No wonder her skin was all glowing white just below the eyes. Good show, Alfie, I thought.

She was quite surprised to see me so chirpy after it. From

what I could gather old Harry tended to come over a bit gloomy at those times. And somehow I could imagine how he would be, thinking how he could have trimmed the privet hedge with all the energy he'd wasted. Or maybe he took it all too much to heart.

"I bet you haven't been with many blokes beside Harry," I said to her.

"I haven't been with a single one," she said, her eyes wide open.

"Except me," I said.

"Yes, sorry," she said, "I'd forgot."

It don't take a woman long to forget if it suits her. "Well, it's widened your experience, gal," I says to her. It had too, short as it was. She kept staring at me every time I said anything as though I was a little oracle or something. All in all, she was quite appreciative in her own little way.

They can say what they want about all this fun-and-games leading up to it, but if you ask me straight out I reckon a bloke feels at his best when he goes at it natural and doesn't start thinking about how to prolong the pleasure. She hadn't mentioned the word precaution and it suited me to think she knew her own business best. So we walked along the towpath together, hand in hand. I wouldn't normally have put my hand into a bird's hand at a time like that – I get this feeling of needing to take my bearings again, but I did it for little Lily because I had a feeling she was imagining for the moment she was walking along with old Harry.

So we got back into Ruby's car. I drove quietly along and dropped Lily off at the corner of her street. I even gave her a little kiss on the side of the cheek as she was getting out. After all there's little enough romance in life. She looked quite an attractive little Mum as she tripped off, and I thought to myself, that was my good deed done for that day.

About two months later I get this letter in the post signed "Lily". Who the bleeding hell's Lily? I thought. I know that name. It's a very short letter and she says she's got to see me. She'd dead scared of the neighbours and of her Mum-in-law who only lives round the next road, in case they should find out. So I drop her a quick line back and tell her to meet me at Lyons' Corner House at the Marble Arch.

Now if little Lily had done a murder she couldn't have been more moggadored, because there's no way out for her. "What you worrying about?" I says, "old Harry will forgive you if you tell him the truth." And she says: "It's not only him – it's his Mum and his family. They'll all know that he can't be the father, because he's been lying on his back in the sanatorium this past six months." Then it seems there's all her relations, and of course the neighbours, and even if Harry wanted to forgive her, he couldn't afford to. They'll all be whispering about how she was having it off while her poor husband was lying helpless in bed in the sanatorium. Yeh, it seems that her little life is going to come to a sad end all because of about three minutes on the grass on a Sunday afternoon when she forgot herself. "Blimey," I said, "thank God I got no relations to consider and I can live my own life just as it comes and goes." So out of kindness I agrees to help her, and lay it all on. There's lots of these tailoring blokes around London willing to earn a crafty few quid.

CHAPTER TWENTY-FOUR

WHEN Lily came back into the room it was hard to believe she was the same woman I'd been lying on the grass with aside of old Father Thames. I mean all the worries and troubles of a woman in her situation had settled round her face. They don't improve a face. I began to wish I'd listened to the little man on my shoulder.

"I've got the money," she said, dipping into her handbag. "Thirty pounds, all in ones, just like you said. Here you are – for when he comes."

I looked down at the notes and the thought crossed my mind that it couldn't have been easy for her to rustle that lot together. The idea even struck me that it would have been a nice little stroke if I pushed the money back into her handbag and said, "This is on me, gal." But as a matter of fact I couldn't. I'd met one geezer the day before who had an old secondhand Riley for sale and he wanted a hundred and ten quid for it. I'd knocked him down to ninety-five, for although there isn't a good sale for that kind of car, I knew if I got one of these student types interested I'd get a hundred and fifty for it. Anyway that had more or less cleaned me out of ready.

"Don't give it to me," I said. "Here, when I ask for it pretend you've only got twenty-five, if you see what I mean. He'll not go back once he's here. And he might have more mercy, if you've got the money."

I was also a bit windy in case anything did go wrong, you can never be sure, so I said to her: "Remember, Lily, this has got nothing to do with me. I'm just helping you out as a friend. That'll put me in the clear. Got me, gal?"

She nodded. You don't like bringing up that side of it at a time like that, but what good will it do to have you doing porridge and she's pushing up the daisy roots? After that we somehow ran out of chat, and I was glad when I heard a knock on the door. "I expect this'll be him, now, Lily," I said, "the medical pranktitioner, as they call him." I went and opened the door.

I'd never seen the chap, although I'd had him described to me by the bloke who put me on to him. I'd even had to telephone him at a certain telephone box because he was that scared of his telephone being tapped, or being trapped by the police. Well, he was a big chap, about forty-five, with horn-rims, and he wore a long dark overcoat, a trilby hat, and to look at him he could have been a National Assistance supervisor, or an embalmer.

He came straight in when I opened the door, but he never said a word. The first thing he did after having a quick look at us both, was to look round the room. He went under the bed, behind doors, into a wardrobe. I was mystified for the minute until it struck me that he must have been making sure the law wasn't in hiding.

"Well, here we are," I said at last, when he'd finally stopped prying about.

"What do you mean," he said, "here we are?"

I know you've got to be cautious in that line of business,

but I did feel he was coming it a bit strong.

"I mean you're at the right place," I said to him. "This is Mrs. Clamacraft," I said, "the young lady what I told you about."

"No names," he said, "no names."

Lily put out her hand and said: "Pleased to meet you." I suppose under the circumstances it was true but it sounded a bit funny to my ear. He seemed in two minds about shaking her hand but then he must have decided there could be no harm in it, and he gave it a polite touch. We all three stood there. Lily didn't know what to say and it was obvious he wasn't going to say anything. He was letting us make all the moves. If there was a hidden microphone anywhere he wasn't going to commit himself on it.

"Have you got your gear with you?" I said.

"Gear?" he said.

"Well you know," I said, "your –" I didn't like coming out with the word *instruments* in front of Lily.

He didn't answer.

"Right," I said, trying a new tack. "I'll go out whilst you examine the young lady, or I could go into the kitchen in case you need me."

He seemed to take the huff at this. "Why should I examine this lady?" he said.

"You've got to, ain't you," I said, "before you do it."

"Before I do what?" he said. He was a real old slyboots.

Lily couldn't make out what all the performance was in aid of. "Be quiet, Alfie," she said. "There must be some mistake."

"Steady up, gal," I said. He was getting me a bit needled. "You are the bloke," I said, "– the gentleman I spoke to on the telephone on Thursday night, aren't you?"

He doesn't say a single dickybird one way or another, and Lily turns to me: "Alfie, be careful – or we'll get into trouble."

This geezer takes a good look at Lily, and he doesn't need telling that she's not acting. He seems to relax a bit then and he speaks to Lily in a very nice way.

"Don't worry my dear," he tells her. "Just sit down on

the chair there and calm yourself." Then he turns to me, "Sit down," he says.

Once he's got us both sitting down he puts his hands behind his back. "Now I must have a serious talk with you both," he says. "Are you two married?"

"Us two married!" I said. "No, definitely not. She's a married woman but I'm a single man."

He begins to pace about, stopping now and again to take a sharp look at us.

"Is there any chance of you two marrying in the future?" he said.

"I very much doubt it," I said. "What do you say, Lily?"

Lily didn't speak. Some things are not even worth an answer.

"But you are the putative father?" he said to me. He seemed to have it in for me.

"The what!" I said. "Who – me, I'm nothing. I'm just obliging a friend. Isn't that so, Lily?"

Lily nodded. For a minute it seemed that her mind was far away.

"I find that very hard to imagine," he said, looking hard at me. His eyes had this way of boring into you. It was worse than being in the dock. I can see he's as good as calling me a liar, but I don't feel it's worth arguing about.

Lily suddenly turned to him: "You are the man who is going to help me?" she said.

"Her old man is in a sanatorium," I said, "and she's had a moral lapse if you see what I mean. Now she's turned to me because she had no one else to turn to. I knew her husband, see. Isn't that so, Lily? It won't never happen again – I can promise you that." Why the hell I should be promising him anything I do not know – after all he'd come to do a job and earn himself thirty nicker. "Now the reason she needs helping out is because her marriage would look very dodgy if her husband was to come out at this stage of the game," I said. "Or to stay in for that matter. He'd know, see. And she's got three other kids as well. Now you've got it all in a nutshell."

"Where do you come into it?" he said.

"I'm just obliging her as a friend," I said. "She'd no place to go."

I could see there was nothing under the sun would ever make him believe me. And it made me mad to feel how unfair he was to me, because I *could* have been helping her out. He's not to know of our swift session on the grass that Sunday afternoon. It might give you a lot of pleasure, but it certainly causes you some pain. This geezer was enjoying the cross-examination, I felt.

"I hope you both realise the seriousness of this case," he began. He was talking to us both but he was eyeing me. "To terminate a pregnancy after more than twenty-eight days is a criminal offence – punishable in a court of law by seven years' imprisonment. Do you both understand?"

This was the last thing I was expecting – to be talked at like this. I'd done my best. I felt like calling the whole thing off there and then.

"I see what you mean," I said. I found I was moving over to his side. It felt to me like Lily was causing a lot of trouble. Not that she could help it.

He began pacing up and down again: "Not only that," he said, "but it's a crime against the unborn child. It's a sin against Nature. It's a course never to be embarked upon lightly." He knew how to preach, I'll say that for him. He left you with nothing to say.

"Therefore," he went on, "I must ask you to consider all the circumstances thoroughly before you go through with it. Since afterwards it will be too late to change your minds."

All I wanted at that moment was to get them both out of my place. I can see I've made a big mistake getting myself involved at all. I've always found that if you leave people alone in this life they'll always work their own way out. It doesn't do to interfere at all.

He looked at Lily after a great long pause: "Have you given the matter your fullest consideration?" he said.

Lily looked at him: "I've no way out," she said. She hadn't either.

"And you wish to go through with it?" he said.

I thought I noticed a touch of relief in his voice, as though he had been afraid for a moment that he might have over-played his hand.

"Yes, I must," said Lily, "I must find someone to do it – if you won't."

I think he enjoyed that little stroke. His face stayed solemn, but not as severe.

"Then I might be able to help you," he said.

"Oh, thank you, thank you very much," said Lily.

Take it easy, gal, I thought – after all, you are paying him.

He began to take his big coat off. As he do I spot a poacher's pocket inside. Sticking out the top of it was a brown instrument case. His entire manner changed, and he looked like a parson who has come down out of the pulpit, and is going to get on with the service without any further messing about. He turned to me. "Now have you got the money?" he said.

"Eh! Oh the money?" I said. "The young lady has it."

"It'll be forty pounds," he said.

"*Forty!*" cried Lily.

"Just a minute," I said. "Thirty pounds is what I under-stood. That's what you always charge."

He hesitated for a second and then said: "Very well, give me thirty. But it should really be forty."

Lily opened her bag and made to hand me the money. I quickly slipped five pounds of it back into the bag and began to count the rest. I thought to myself: if he can go down ten, he can go down another five.

"Lily," I said. "You've only twenty-five pounds here. Is that all you've got gal?" I turned to him: "I could let you have the other five tomorrow."

"Out of the question," he said. And I can see he meant it.

He stands there and waits, and Lily tries to dip into her bag to salvage the other five notes, but I stop her. I take my last fiver out of my pocket and put it with the twenty five and hand it over to him. He gets hold of the roll like a bank clerk and counts it quickly but very carefully. It's not the first time he's counted a bundle of notes. Then he puts it into his back pocket and carefully fastens the flap button down. Short of slicing the pocket right out with a razor blade, the whizz mob would have had a hard job getting it.

Once he'd got hold of that money his manner got very brisk, and all sign of the preaching parson vanished. "I'll use the bed in that other room," he said. "Have you got the brown paper?"

"Yes," I said, "four sheets."

"I shall need some boiling water and a clean bowl," he said.

"Right," I said, "I'll get it for you out of the kitchen. I won't be long."

Now that the time has come Lily turns a bit nervous, she goes silent and pale. This geezer seems to spot it and for a moment he looks quite human.

"Don't worry, my dear," he tells her. "Come along with me."

Lily picks up this little canvas bag in which she has her things and lets him lead her across the room and into the other room. He gave one look at me and then closed the door.

CHAPTER TWENTY-FIVE

I FELT choked to see old Lily going into the room with that bloke. I didn't even know his name. I'd been told to ask for Mr. Smith, but that wasn't his real name. It was only when he went out of the room and I was able to think in cold blood, that I tumbled him for the taker-on he was. His preachifying had struck clean home, whilst he was doing it, but once he'd turned his back I realized what it was all put there for. "It's a crime against the unborn child – it's a course never to be embarked upon lightly – examine your consciences –". It was an act, but the sort of act he could salve his own conscience with, if you see what I mean. He'd begun to believe himself. Then at the same time he was preparing his defence in advance in case he made a slip. All that he'd said to us would sound very good in a court of law – all except the money bit. I could see him telling the judge: "Not my fault that she died, my Lord – I begged them not to do it. I appealed to their consciences. I only helped them in case the woman attempted anything herself, and worse should happen. The woman said she would have to find someone."

I'll bet he gives them that spiel at every house he goes to – he was word perfect. It was all a load of cobblers. His true self came out when he said: "*Have you got the money?*" You should have seen the look that came into his eyes then. I wonder what it is about money that seems to get into people's blood. We all like it, but it has got some people really in its clutches. "Twenty five! out of the question – I must have thirty." And to think I never tumbled him at the start.

The kettle began to boil and I went to the door and whispered: "Your water's boiling". He came in with his sleeves rolled up, carrying his instrument case. "A saucepan," he said.

As luck would have it Annie had bought a new saucepan and I'd never used it since she went, so it was spotless clean. He rinsed it out and then took out a big syringe, put it in the saucepan, poured the boiling water over it and put it back on the gas ring and let it boil away. Then he got my plastic bowl, rinsed it out with hot water, poured more hot water in, added some Dettol, and began to scrub, scour and wash it clean. Actually, it was quite clean when he started. But not clean enough for him. When he had finally got it to his satisfaction he put a new lot of hot water into it, some more Dettol, then got a piece of his own soap, his own nail brush, and began to scrub up his hands. And the way he went at them you wouldn't think they were his own.

He was in no hurry, by the looks of things, and he went on scrubbing and scrubbing his nails and his hands until I felt he'd scrub the skin off. When at last he'd finished he got his own little towel out and he wiped his hands scrupulously clean. I mean he went round the nails and the finger-tips and one thing and another until I'll bet there wasn't a cleaner pair of hands in London. I don't think he cared for me watching him. Then he finished off by waving them about in the air to dry them. Then he emptied the bowl, rinsed it out, poured some more hot water in, added some cold, put some Dettol in, and blow me down if he don't start washing his maulers all over again.

Know what, he only repeated the operation three times. Talk about a nut case. I was that ashamed for him that after the second time I pretended I didn't even notice. What the hell can he be washing away? I thought. On top of which you could hear this syringe bobbing up and down in the saucepan like he was boiling lobsters for lunch. And whilst this was going on I began to wonder why a bachelor man like myself ever has anything to do with a woman, because you've got to admit it's a messy business from start to finish. I'd always thought what sorry sods queers are, how they're missing out on the love stakes, never to know the lovely soft feel of a woman's body, but as I watched this bloke scrubbing and wiping away, and I thought of little Lily lying on the bed, I could at least understand there were certain troubles they were saved.

When he'd finally finished he fishes the syringe out with a pair of tongs, and he asks me to put some more hot water in the handbowl in case he wants to wash his hands again, and some Dettol and the rest of it, and bring it into the other room. So I do all this and I go in. I was quite surprised to see how he'd got his stall decked out. On a chair was a paper with a white cloth over it, and his syringe and things. On the bed there's a rubber sheet and a white cloth partly over it. Lily, wearing a little thin dressing gown, is lying on the bed. I put the bowl of hot water and Dettol on a low chest of drawers. "You have locked the door?" he said.

"What door?" I said.

"The door," he said, "lock and bolt it so that nobody can come in."

Then he went to the window and spied out making sure nobody could look in. There was a great big empty derelict bombed area never been rebuilt, so he was quite safe, but even that didn't satisfy him. He went and half pulled the curtains across.

"Lock the door at once," he said, "and bolt it. Don't let anybody in." He wasn't a bloke to argue with so I went out of the room, closed the door and then locked and bolted the other door.

CHAPTER TWENTY-SIX

WHAT was I doing there? To be frank, I didn't know. I'm the same as any other man where women are concerned, I'm only interested in the pleasure. When it comes to the pain I just don't want to know. You can't blame me – you can only blame human nature. Well, they are mysterious things are women. I mean the closer you come to look at them. I mean if the thing that happens to them every month were to happen to me only once in my lifetime, I'd feel like drowning myself. But they don't seem to mind, they take it all in their stride. Then take when they're pregnant, what a horrible idea that is, some little thing inside you, kicking about for months on end, then popping out head first, could be nine or ten pound weight, and he's no sooner born than he sticks his mouth on a nipple and sucks the life out of you. And yet they seem to actually enjoy it. So you've got to admit there's a gulf between man and woman.

And some of the things a poor woman has to let a man do to her. Just to keep in his good books, you could say. I mean I could go on endless. But as for a man, he's simple, all he's got is pretty much on the surface, or at least ninety per cent of it. In a way I suppose that's why we're nothing compared with a woman, I mean for things going on inside us. And I'll stay nothing, I will for sure. Who'd be a woman? Course, I suppose if you're born that way you know no better. They're more to be pitied than blamed. It makes you understand how most of them are just that bit bonkers.

I suddenly heard this cry of pain in the next room. It wasn't a loud one, but it frightened me. It was a sudden sharp cry. I heard him whisper something to her in his deep voice. I will say this for him, he certainly had the manner. He gave you the impression he knew what he was doing of. Mind you, I hate any instruments touching me. It used to take all my discipline at the start to let old Daphne trim my corns. I heard another cry, and then I heard him talking to her again. Poor Lily – they can say what they want, but life is definitely loaded against the woman.

It all hadn't taken three minutes, and she'd spent as many months worrying, and twenty-five pound in the bargain to wipe out the memory. No, not the memory, I mean the consequences. I'd have to do something about that money perhaps. And now she had to undergo this lot on top of it. A bloke like that messing about with syringes and things. I never got used to that game even when I was in the sanatorium. And they always tried to tell you it won't hurt. I went and filled the kettle and put it on the stove and at the same time I caught a glimpse of my face in the little mirror by the sink: You're a right cowson, Alfie, I said to myself. It's a thing you should know what it means – it means you've forgiven yourself for being one.

It went quiet for a bit in the next room, and the door opened and this geezer came in. I was surprised to see he'd been sweating. It was there on his forehead, this little film of sweat. He was in a bit of a hurry this time, wiping his hands with the little towel, and letting down his shirt-sleeves. I heard a very faint moan come from inside. I was going to ask him how it was all getting on when he said: "I say, could you make some tea?"

"Tea," I said, "yeh, I'll make some tea." I thought to myself – he wants tea on the job now, why, with what he's earning he could afford champagne. No income tax, see. "It won't be long," I said, "the kettle's almost boiling."

"Oh I shan't be staying for it," he said. "It's for the young lady. She'll need it rather strong with plenty of sugar in."

He wouldn't be staying – what did he mean? Was he going out for a pint or something.

"Why aren't you staying," I said. "Have you done?"

"Almost all I can do," he said, and he began putting his gear away. In spite of his official manner I could see he was in a dead hurry to get away.

"That didn't take you very long," I said. "Can she go home when she's had her cup of tea?" Blimey, they do earn their money easy, I thought.

He looked up at me as he was putting his case carefully

148

away inside the poacher's pocket in his big overcoat, which he hadn't yet put on.

"Good gracious no!" he said. "On no account must she go off." He came up to me and looked at me as though I were a nut: "Don't you understand? – it's only been induced. It hasn't happened, all that's to come." He looked at me again and I thought the idea crossed his mind that somebody so dim as that couldn't be so bad. I thought he softened a bit. A mistake on his part, see, because you only put yourself in the wrong when you do that. He dipped his fingers into his waistcoat pocket and pulled out a tiny bottle. "By the way, should her temperature rise give her two of these tablets. I'll leave you six. But two should be enough."

I looked at the tablets. "How will I know if it rises?" I said. He now looked at me as if I was real dumb, but after all, how are you to know? I didn't have one of those thermometer things to stick in the mouth, and anyway I can never read one of them things.

"If she sweats a great deal, or feels flushed and hot," he said very slowly, "give her two tablets with some cold water."

"I see," I said. But I wasn't letting him off that easy. "Suppose something goes wrong?" I said.

"Nothing should go wrong," he said.

"But suppose it do," I said. "Can I get in touch with you?"

"No, you can't," he said. I thought he was quite emphatic about that. He looked at me and said: "In a case of emergency there's only one thing – get a cab and get her to the nearest hospital." He was already standing at the door, unbolting and unlocking it. "You simply say she's had a haemorrhage. They're very understanding. But of course, I'm not expecting you'll have any trouble."

"Just a minute, mate," I said, "don't you think you should see the job through – considering how much you've been paid?"

He looked at me and for the first time I saw a genuine look or something come to his face: "I was afraid that manner would come out before I left," he said. He looked quite human.

"What manner?" I said.

"They almost go down on their knees when I arrive," he said, "pleading they'll commit suicide if I don't help them. In nine cases out of ten they find they're short of money. But when I've done my job, and I'm ready to leave, they change very suddenly."

Know what, I almost felt sorry for the poor geezer. Of course I didn't let him see it. Same as I say, never let anybody see you're sorry – it puts you even more in the wrong. "Do it surprise you?" I said.

"No, it doesn't," he said. "Nothing surprises me any more. Two if she sweats."

He opened the door and slipped away dead silently. He's unhappy, I thought. He's one of those who love money, but don't like themselves for loving it. I heard a little sigh, and to my surprise there was Lily, hobbling in through the door, her hands in the dressing-gown pockets.

"What are you doing of?" I said.

"I've got to keep on the move," she said.

"How you feeling, gal?" I said.

She went round the room without saying anything. I went and made the tea. While I was waiting for it to brew I handed her the tablets: "He said for you to take two of these if your temperature rises. If you feel very hot or sweating."

I poured her a cup of tea out and put plenty of sugar and milk in. I gave it to her and she took one big greedy gulp at it, as though she were thirsty. Her face seemed to have come over white and waxy.

"Blimey, you do look old, gal," I said to her. You've got to show a bit of sympathy. And she seemed to have put years on. She never said anything to that. "He got his money easy," I said.

"I owe you five pounds," she said, going to her bag.

"You owe me nothing," I said.

"I'd rather pay you," she said.

"If you *insist*," I said, "I'll take it. But to be quite frank, I'd rather you didn't." I put her bag down.

She must have had other things on her mind, because she didn't bother one way or another, and I was glad she didn't. She did look ropey. "Are you sure you're all right?" I said. She didn't answer. She put her cup down and I filled it again. "I'd hate for anything to happen here," I said. I was thinking about the seven years he'd said was the sentence. I know it sounds a rotten thing to think, but it was uppermost in my mind.

Suddenly she let out a loud moan of pain. It scared me. It was that long and deep it seemed not to come from her mouth but from right away inside her.

"Sh, sh," I said, "not so loud, Lily."

We sat there a bit longer, then she got to her feet and began to hobble about, bending now and again. I thought: I've got to get myself out of here. There was nothing I could do. I know it sounds bad, but it's different when they're there beside you, in pain, and there's nothing you can do. She let out another moan, a real loud one.

"Quiet, gal," I whispered. I didn't want anybody to hear.

She turned on me: "I can't help it – you fool," she cried out at me. "Don't you understand – I'm in pain – I'm in pain – and I can't help it."

I thought I've got to do it now or it'll be too late. So I felt myself draw my hand back and give her a good hard slap across the cheek. Not too hard, but it was harder than I'd intended. It made a loud slapping sound, and she went dead quiet.

"Don't look at me like that," I said in a loud whisper. "I didn't want to do it, but I had to. You were getting hysterical. You sounded like a wild animal. The bloke from down below might have dropped in, or one of the neighbours. And what do you think would have happened? – you'd have had the police here, and the ambulance, and they would have carted you off. Then all this that you've gone through would have been for nothing. You'd have been found out." The shock of the slap was wearing off and she was feeling the pain. "Don't look at me like that," I said.

I'd gone very calm, but I could feel she'd have me hysterical if I was to stay around any longer. I went and got my jacket and put it on.

She looked at me. "You're not going," she said. "You're not going to leave me, Alfie." She even got hold of my sleeve.

"You'll be better on your own," I said. "It's one of them things where nobody can help you – and you've got to suffer it out on your own. Let go, Lily, and don't look at me like that, as if I wasn't human. I could flannel you, but where would it get us? If the pain comes on hard – stick a pillow in your mouth. That'll drown the sound."

She wasn't for letting me go, and though I didn't fancy playing my last card I had to: "Listen," I said, "think of old Harry – of Harry and the kids." When I said that she let go of me. I crept quietly out of the room.

CHAPTER TWENTY-SEVEN

I WENT out into the Sunday street. Two kids were going about with red plastic buckets and sponges. "Wash your car, mister?" said one. "Some other time," I said. "There might be no other time," said one of them. The things they come out with. I got into the car and drove off.

That's one good thing you can say about a car – you can go out on the roads amongst people but nobody can get at you in any way. You're shielded off. The most they can do is honk their horn, which you can ignore, or they might give you a look but you don't have to see that look if you don't want to. In fact, the secret of driving in London is never to catch any other driver's eye. Whatever you do, never look at him when one of you has to give way – especially if he's a cab-driver. Pretend you're dead ignorant. Then they have to give way. You take a dead stupid nit of a woman driver, crossing one way with her blinker going the other – they all get out of her way.

But to get back to what I was saying – your contact is all over and done with in a couple of seconds when you're in your own car, and you've got these windscreens and things in between you. But you go out walking and everybody you pass can have a good gander at you. For that one reason, if for no other, the car manufacturers can't go wrong in the future. Who wants to meet people if they can possibly avoid it? If you know a car-owner, ask him how long it is since he went on a bus or had a good walk round a town.

I could have gone and had a beer up at a duff sort of Sunday lunchtime strip club I know, but I'm not that sort of bloke. I can't bear to be in the company of blokes who go for strippers and all that schoolboy stuff. And the last thing I want when I'm feeling real sad is to go and get drunk. I like to think my way through things or feel them or something of the sort, until I come to the cheery part. I mean the only experience that doesn't do you any good is the one you learn nothing from.

Now I didn't know where I was going, and you're a nuisance on the roads when you're like that. So where do I find myself but over in Battersea Park along by the little miniature railway there. You get a few deer hanging about there behind the railings. It's all around where I used to take Malcolm on Sunday mornings. So I parked the car and I get out to have a walk round.

Somehow I didn't fancy going over the same ground again, I mean the old ground, so I went along by the embankment towpath towards Albert Bridge, just beside the Pleasure Gardens. The wind was blowing from the West so that you didn't get the smoke from Battersea Power Station – *washed* smoke they call it, but have you ever tasted it! – so I did a few of my deep breathing exercises along the way. Oh but what a horrible idea of those who ever thought of them as pleasure gardens. It's all a take-on. You wouldn't get me going in there. I must say you get a real bunch of nits going there. I mean if I ever hear of anybody going there or to Madame Tussaud's it makes me feel dead uncomfortable.

I kept thinking of little Lily. It's funny what women have to go through in this life. There were lots of people strolling along, but none of my sort. I was the odd man out. You get a different kind of person troops about in each different part of London. You get people in Green Park have never set foot in Battersea Park and vice versa. It's a funny thing, but on Sundays in St. James's Park you seem to get lots of people from the East End. I suppose the Tubes have a lot to do with it. You get Londoners going to Kensington Gardens would never dream of crossing the Serpentine bridge and going into Hyde Park. Now in Hyde Park you get a very cosmopolitan lot – Irish, Italians, Bubbles – a real mixed bunch. As for Regent's Park, they're mostly all one lot who go there from Golders Green way, but that's around the tea house and the Queen Mary rose garden. If you go up towards the playing fields south of the Zoo you'll get people from Camden Town and other parts. It's all very well ordered by the people themselves. They do keep themselves apart, I will say that for them.

Now I'm the sort of bloke who gets a terribly lonely feeling, in which I can't bear to see anybody, and I've got to be alone, when suddenly it wears itself out, and I find I'm longing for a bit of company. I mean an hour of myself when I'm like that and I've had enough of my own company. Now the first thing I did think of is of slipping into the car and nipping across to see Ruby. Only five minutes away across Chelsea Bridge and down there along by the Embankment. Or across Albert Bridge for that matter. But I had told her I was going out to see Harry at the sanatorium, and I didn't want to drop in on her too early. Not only that, but it's a funny time to call on a bird – about two o'clock on a Sunday afternoon – I mean if you've had no dinner. After all, what do you do? And I didn't feel hungry.

It suddenly struck me I could do worse than ring Daphne, this chiropodist woman from Dr. Brown's. She was a very settling sort of woman in many ways. And she made a handsome cup of tea. I always say, Spinsters for tea – it means more to them, see. On top of which I had a little corn needed attention, and my toenails needed a good trim. I'd only visited her once since I came out of the sanatorium but she was always glad to see me. And she'd bring out her tin of Ormskirk gingerbreads, and a stale bit of a Lyons' Swiss Roll. But same as I say, people like that can make them things taste good – or nearly. It'll kill two birds with one stone, I thought. I mean if there was none of the other coming old Daphne would settle for a cuddle and a few old jokes. To be quite frank, I didn't feel like knocking myself out with old Rube just at that exact moment.

So I go to a telephone kiosk and I ring her up and right enough she answered. So I chat her up with one or two jokes before she has the sense to tell me she has her sister with her who'll be staying for tea. But it would be fine if I called round about six o'clock. Those clots of spinsters can waste a bloke's time. In fact, whether she had her sister there or not I wouldn't know, but I can't see why she would want to tell me a lie. You know what you can do with your sister, I thought. And yourself, too, come to that. So I cut the chat dead short.

Now just as I've put the receiver down, and I'm giving my hair a comb before going out into the world, I look through the window of the kiosk, and for a second or two I think I'm seeing a mirage or something. There's this kid going by who's the dead spit of little Malcolm. He's older, of course, and bigger, but he runs just like him and he looks just like him. *Christ, it is Malcolm!* I go all flurried inside when I see him. Now when he's gone past I get this impulse to push the door open and hurry out and look after him, but lucky I don't. Because the next thing a bloke and a woman go tripping by. She's carrying this little baby, see, all wrapped up in christening shawls and that. I saw the face as it went by – I mean the woman's face. It wasn't looking in my direction, in fact it wasn't looking in any direction. It was mostly looking down on this child in its arms. It took a full second to strike home who it was – it was little Gilda.

She hadn't half suffered a sea change. She looked real respectable. To be quite frank, she looked as though in a year or two she might turn out dumpified. She had the look of a woman who's getting *everything* regular – I don't mean just the one thing. Meals, money, new gas stoves – and some of the other. Though she could be going short weight if anything on that. But that's not to say it's troubling her at this moment. Her mind is full of this new baby and the christening. In tow with her she has this geezer Humphrey. He won't mind her going dumpy. In fact some men prefer that kind of woman. That's what keeps the world going – each man fancies a different bird. There's hope for every woman unless she loses heart. And they only do that when they're full of themselves. Don't let 'em kid you.

Humphrey's all decked out in his best charcoal grey suit (they've gone completely out of fashion, but he's not to know that), and he's walking along like a man who's found a dream come true. Behind them is this couple, who might have been his brother and wife or something of the sort. They all look dead close to each other. "You won't never leave us, Alfie," she had said. "I'll make it up to you." She made it up all right. Still, you can't blame 'em – they've got to think of themselves first. But they shouldn't make out to be any different.

They went by. I stood there for a minute to get over it. They must have been married about three months when he popped her one in the oven, I thought – well, you know how you work these dates out. Then I went out of the kiosk and watched after them. I could see there was no chance of them spotting me. They wouldn't have noticed me if I'd been standing there in my pelt. They had eyes only for themselves, for the new baby and for what they were doing. I wanted to get another glimpse of Malcolm. I saw Humphrey hold his hand out and Malcolm took hold of it. Funny, I wasn't jealous. I was glad. If you actually love someone you don't want harm or suffering come to them. I suppose on that score you could say that child was the only person I'd love for himself. I saw them go into the churchyard and into the church.

I walked off in the opposite direction. I thought I'd better be getting back to Lily, see how she's getting on. What was it he said to me – never is a long time. He was right. Then when I got near the bridge on my way back I kept thinking how I'd like to have another look at little Malcolm. There was no reason why I couldn't go and have a look at him. So I went back. After all he was my child. My child – what does that mean? One bloke told me – I think it was Sharpey – that either he saw it on television or he read it in a newspaper, that there's about five million seeds spurt out of a man at one good go, and any one of that lot could be his child. So what does it boil down to? I don't know what it boils down to. Facts are facts and feelings are feelings, I suppose.

Now the hardest part was to screw up enough courage to go into the church. But I needn't have worried, there was nobody about. They don't seem to flock into those places no more. I don't believe they even go to bed no more on Sunday afternoons. They all watch television. It was quite a lovely little church. I mean it had an air of peace about it. I should say it was a bit High Church from the looks of things. It's got lighted candles and that. So I creep in and I stand there at the back, out of the way behind a pillar, and I see they're all gathered in a little group round what you call a font or something. There's this priest or minister or somebody, he's putting water and stuff on the kid's head and saying prayers over it – something about how he's got to renounce the devil and all that sort of thing. And these other two behind, what they call the Godparents, have to speak up for him on the side of God. I quite liked that little bit about the devil and God. I think the sooner you get all that into a kid's head the sooner he'll know where he stands. After all, each one of us, we need somebody to turn to in this life. I mean it's not so much whether you do right or wrong, in my opinion, but that you know the difference between them. I do detest it when there's somebody around who don't know one thing from the other. It seems to cut them off from you.

Anyway, I've got my eye on little Malcolm as he is watching on. I couldn't believe how he had grown. And yet I expected him to be taller. Then he decides to have a nosey round the place. Same as I say, I was standing behind this pillar, and I thought I'd better get out of his way. Then I can see he's spotted there's somebody there – so I stick to my ground. He comes along and he looks up at me. This parson bloke is still going on about the devil. I kind of smile at him, not like I used to do, I put more of a grin on my face and give him a wink. I was afraid he might shout out *"Daddy"* or something. That would have made a stir. But his face didn't change. I mean the expression. He looked at me the way a rich kid will mostly look at you – never a smile, not even a blink, just a dead cool stare.

Know what, that child didn't know me from Adam!

CHAPTER TWENTY-EIGHT

I KEPT thinking now and again about Lily. Well, not what you could call *thinking*, more like little thoughts of her would keep crossing my mind. I sometimes think if only thoughts would leave me alone my life could be happy. But I felt I didn't want to go back there just yet. The fact was, I had more need of some comfort myself just then than of handing it out. Anyway, I do drive back and turn down the street. Same as I told myself, duty is duty. I was half expecting to see an ambulance there, and people gathered about the door, and perhaps the law with a notebook. But as it happened it was all peaceful and quiet. I thought to myself – you'd never think walking along a street what can be happening behind those doors and windows.

Anyway, I kept the wheels turning. She's either gone or she's still there, I thought, but in any case what can I do? I knew it looked bad, but then you don't mind how bad a thing looks providing you're the only one who knows about it. After all, he's a poor bloke who can't find an excuse for himself. And another thing – what don't look bad when you get close up against it? Ever heard anybody in Court answer a solicitor about exactly what they did in a certain situation? You could be an innocent man, yet when you go into details he'll make you sound like a real villain. Course it's his job. Still, I'll admit it didn't look nice to drive past.

I'm crossing Lambeth Bridge when I suddenly have an idea, and I go down Horseferry Road instead of turning along the Embankment, and as I pass Westminster Hospital there's this woman outside selling flowers from a barrow, as I knew there would be. Now here's a handy tip, if ever you want to buy flowers on a Sunday in London; keep away from Victoria or the Marble Arch, they'll fiddle you for sure. Make for a hospital, there's always somebody selling flowers outside and they won't gyp you. A fair profit but no more. Mind you, I think flowers are nearly all profit. I bought her one dozen lovely yellow roses. I was going to buy red, but then I felt I'd better not come it too strong. I got the woman to put lots of paper round them, the very best she's got, and pin the wrapping down at the top. She even offered me a Cellophane wrapper she'd got hold of, but somehow that stuff reminds me of funerals, so I turned it down.

But fancy Malcolm not recognising me! I couldn't get over that. Same as I say, he didn't know me from Adam. Or could it have been he did and thought he'd better say nothing? Or perhaps he recognised me but couldn't place me. They've got funny memories have kids. Here, a mate of mine called Danny had come into a few quid one time – pools I think it was, or it might have been the dogs – and he let his old woman persuade him that she was near a breakdown and that she needed a fortnight's rest without the kid. Danny's own mum only brought twelve of them up, and never had a holiday in her life, but same as they say, other times other customs. He's a youngster of three this kid, so they put him into a private nursery for the time – very expensive place it was, about twelve quid a week. Course it rained all the fortnight – I think it was Brighton they went to – and old Danny was dead miserable all the time longing to see the kid, see. Then they nipped over to pick him up on the Sunday evening – only two weeks later – and know what, that kid made out he didn't know them! He screamed his head off, and clung tight to the Matron, and he begged of her to send them away. It gave old Danny the biggest shock he'd ever had. That kid was his sun and moon, and here he is after a fortnight and he don't want to know. Well finally they had to pull him off – and the Matron didn't want him to go, for after all Matrons are human as well. Anyway this kid screamed and cried all the way back home in the car. So Danny's old woman threatened what she'd do to him if he didn't belt up. Then Danny blew his top proper: "If you so much as lay a finger on him," he warned her, "I'll chop your bleeding head off your shoulders." And he told me he would have done too, he was that upset himself. He reckoned it took months for the kid to come round. So there you are.

As I'm driving along towards Thompson Court I find I start planning my future in my mind. Very unusual for me, because I mostly like to live a day at a time, but I feel the time has come round for me to settle down. I think I must have had a bit of a shaking up during the course of the day, see. Yes, I'm definitely going to settle down with this Ruby, I decide. Thinking it over, I've had enough of being on the move; somehow I find I'm not stalking these young birds any more. I mean I'm going in more for comfort. Well, after all, comfort is something you can enjoy when you're ninety. (I'm telling myself all this, see.) You get a young bird and you can bet certain for sure she'll keep bringing up love. But Ruby hardly ever mentions the word. Perhaps it'll slip out at just the rare moment instead of one of the other short words. Same as I say, she knows what she wants. You get the same with most older birds, you'll hear 'em say: *Aren't we having a good time!* They don't keep going on about love and getting engaged. They know the score. Here, I'd one mature woman one time, a grave digger's widow, see, I was in digs with her – never charged me except for my laundry, and she used to say: "Go with who you want, Alfie, and enjoy yourself. But come home to me at night – that's all I ask." They're more appreciative, and same as I say, some of them can't half go to town!

Where was I? Oh yes – Ruby. Another thing – she always has plenty of food and drink in, gins, whiskies, you name it and she has it, except perhaps Dimple Haig, but who wants that – whilst these young chicks can't even offer you a glass of Lucozade. Comfort never enters a young bird's mind. Not unless she's a real fat lazy dope. And Ruby's got some beautiful clobber. She goes in mostly for what you call "model" coats, and she's got some lovely fur coats as well, a real Persian Lamb, she's even got a Wild Mink jacket for evenings. And you should see all the fashion cards she's got on her mantelpiece: *Hardy Amies Ltd.*

request the pleasure of your company at the showing of their Spring Collection. Then you get *Worth* requests it, *Paquin, Norman Hartnell* – I don't know how many of those fashion geezers request the pleasure of Ruby's company.

I must say like any other normal man, I love a woman you can take out and show off. It's half the pleasure. I mean it don't half make these other geezers envy you. I once took her to the club where Sharpey and Perce were, and you should have seen their faces. And getting back to domestic things, there's this marvellous big bath she had put in. It's out of this world with all its mirrors. I love it when she gets it all full up, not too hot, but frothy and scented, and we can sit there, splashing and whatnot, and rubbing one another's backs down and having fun. I bet they can hear us laughing in the next flat's bathroom. They must wonder at times what we're up to. I find it very relaxing that sort of thing. It means you can have a lot of fun without absolutely knocking yourself out, if you see what I mean. Well, why extend yourself on every occasion. You've got your health to think of. And of course I always finish off with the old cold shower. Same as I say, it tightens you handsome. But these young birds, why, they can't even offer you a bowl of water to wash your hands in. I'll bet if you got one of them in a bath like Ruby's they'd be lost. Like as not they'd start scrubbing themselves or something of that sort, and make the water all scummy. Same with this bidet she's had specially put in. They wouldn't even know what one of them was for. Although you could hardly make it more obvious. Mind you, they are a bit overfacing for a start – I mean the way they shout it out. It's not the sort of thing you could have in a family house, of course, not with youngsters around. Still, same as old Ruby says: "It takes the French to think of a thing like this." They seem to have thought of quite a lot of things.

CHAPTER TWENTY-NINE

I PARKED my car alongside one of these big squares you get about parts of London with grass and flowers in the middle and trees all round and people walking their dogs around in it – St. George's Square or something they call it. There were two young nuts racing along on these Italian scooters, and they were making a hell of a din, filling the square it was, and I thought how it must have been, say about sixty years before, with only these horse-drawn carriages rolling along, and the nice *clop-clop* of hooves, and no smells except from the odd pile of steaming horse droppings. One old boy I once worked with told me how at one time he used to put the straw down in the streets if any famous man was ill, so that the sound of the carriages going by wouldn't disturb him. They wouldn't do that for anybody in these days. They'd stop outside your front door and blow their bloody horns to hasten you on. I think people must have lost all respect. That's what makes their lives so empty. If they've no respect for others they can't have any for themselves.

Anyway, I nipped round the corner to this Thompson Court. Course I'm keeping the roses well out of sight. I mean somebody has only to spot you walking into a block of flats on a Sunday afternoon with a bunch of flowers and not only do you look a right lemon, but unless they're dead dim they must know for certain what you're after. And you don't want your private intentions open to everybody along the street. I mean, I've often seen one of these civil servant types with his bowler hat and umbrella, taking his old woman a bunch of flowers home of a Friday, and I've spotted from the look in his eyes what's on his mind. I suppose it's the five-day week has done it – he knows he don't have to get up early Saturday morning. Not that I want to run civil servants down. In some ways I think they're the backbone of this country – well, perhaps not the backbone, the coalminers are that, but they're definitely a steadying influence.

I rang the lift bell. There must have been a couple of these old dames using it – one holding the lift door whilst the other was having a good rabbit. The world could come to an end but they'll never cut short a chat. I had a thought cross my mind about the funny thing that happened me on my very first visit to Ruby's flat.

Now I can't say whether it was it being across the river off my usual manor, or the uniformed porters around the block, or poncing about her flat with the thick carpets under my feet, and perfumes I wasn't used to – I don't know what it was – but I didn't feel up to her, if you see what I mean. I'd never struck that high socially. Mind you, we hadn't got cracking, but I had a strong suspicion I would what they call not rise to the occasion.

Of course, that was not the first time it had ever happened to me. I suppose it happens to every normal man some time or other. In fact, on my mind at that very moment – when I could sense things going wrong on my very first visit to Ruby's flat – was a memory of a cracking bit of nukky I came across down at Hastings. Leastways it looked so to me at the time. It's about twenty-two, see, and it's gone there with its aunt, and old Auntie goes off on these mystery coach trips in the afternoon, and this bird goes sunbathing on the beach. Its figure is near dead perfect – it's tall, flat-stomached, light-chested, and long and lean in the leg, hair on the short side. Not really my type, come to that, but I'm always prepared to make an adjustment. If I'm having it off with a short bandy-legged bint I keep telling myself how marvellous bow legs are and asking myself why I don't go in for them more. Same with great big fat birds. Whoever I'm with at the time is my favourite type, if you see what I mean. It's the same as I say, that's what we're here for to make one another happy.

Now I got the impression it was a bit on the sulky side for a start, but it turns out it's only stone deaf in the left ear. It would answer some things I asked it and not others. It had to do with whether it was watching my lips when the tide was making this grunting sound it does over the pebbles.

Anyway, once I'd found out about the left side I took good care I played it up on the right side. I even got it talking, and it went on about a visit it had made to a sewage works somewhere, a long rigmarole it was, all about filter beds, and what it called an activated sludge process. It must have gone on for three or four hours, giving me all the fascinating details of sewage disposal, from the moment you flush the chain on it to how it ends up as dried sludge and is sold so much a ton as fertilizer. During the course of this I slipped from starboard side to port a few times and told it what I thought about it, and its powers of conversation, in no uncertain terms, as they say.

Anyway, come Thursday, (I'd been working hard on it since Monday, double Neapolitans, Coca-cola, lollies, the lot) and I have it out in my car, miles from anywhere, up a disused cart track hidden away on the Sussex Downs.

Now it's been my experience with these shy, dim, stuffy birds, that they can be very much like one of these old pre-war cars, real old bangers, that you can be swinging until your arm nearly drops off, when suddenly they spark, and the engine jumps to life and the whole body starts throbbing and vibrating from the rear light to the front bumper. And it turns out exactly like that with this bird. It wouldn't let me hold its hand one minute – and the next it's all over me. I've never known anything like. Course it's marvellous air up there.

Know what, believe it or not, I wasn't a blind bit of use !

Imagine, something that has plagued you nearly every minute of the day and night since you were twelve, has never let you down once, is as regular as Big Ben, and now you suddenly put it to use in what seems ideal circumstances, and it doesn't want to know. I couldn't believe it at first. Then I didn't know what to do about it. Naturally I kept playing up the hot passion as though I was bursting for it – at the same time underneath I'm racking my brains as to what I should do about it. I kept praying the law would turn up and save the situation. It only goes to show what these poor geezers who are half bent must go through when they ain't sure which way they ought to turn. I would have turned the heater on because a hot draught of engine air up the trouser legs is quite helpful (that's really why these lorry drivers are such a randy lot, it's the hot fumey air rising from the floorboards up their legs, but take them out of their cabs on to the wet grass and they're often useless), but, of course, the heater doesn't work unless you're moving.

Next I tried thinking up all the dirty things I could bring my mind to, filthy postcards and What the Butler saw, but none of that don't work, they just didn't seem filthy any more – bloody comic if anything. So it decides to start trying to help out, but it only makes things far worse. It had a very heavy clumsy, uncertain touch – it turns out it's one of these physiotherapists in a hospital, so you can imagine what they're like. I mean whilst I don't want to say anything against that end of the medical profession, it's a well-known fact that any pain a woman physiotherapist relieves in a man she'll leave two in its place. Finally, there was nothing for it but admit defeat. I mean the way these hard therapist's mitts of hers kept groping about my person I was scared stiff that she might do me an injury. Course I had to make an excuse, and I swore it was the lime juice the barman had put into my light ale caused it. I explained how they gave it to our troops in hot countries abroad to quieten them down; and to the U.S. navy as well. I said I'd go on Mackeson or something next night and there'd be no stopping me. Somehow I couldn't even strike the right level in my chat.

So then I had to drive it home and drop it back at its guest-house where Auntie was waiting for it. And it didn't half give me a dodgy look when I said goodnight. But at least I was able to stare Auntie in the face. So then I drive back, not on speaking terms no more with the old man for having let me down.

I was the last in at the digs, and the landlady, whose husband had run off with one of the washers-up, opened her miserable heart and gave me a crafty cup of cocoa in the kitchen. She wasn't all that much to look at – given to warts in fact, one on the chin and one on the side of her nose – and she had a horrible personality, dead mean – if she'd a couple of gumboils she wouldn't give you one – and yet suddenly I conceived a fantastic passion for her. I don't know how it was, I mean we're sitting in this kitchen, well, it was more of a scullery in fact than a kitchen, and there was this smell of soapsuds and burnt fat hanging about the place, and she was wearing a greasy blouse, an old black shiny skirt, a tattered pinny and an old pair of her husband's slippers and, as I remember, had no stockings on. And yet to me she was like the most sexy young piece on earth, far out beyond any rotten little film star, as she rabbited away about an Autumn holiday she'd once had in Guernsey, Channel Isles, with two lady friends, and she got out an album, showed me about seven million snapshots they'd taken. The funny thing was I wasn't the least bit bored. Perhaps that was because I never seemed to hear a word she said, I was that infatuated by her. I took my jacket off – after asking permission in this husky voice that had come over me – and rolled up my shirtsleeves, just so I could rub the skin of my arms against hers as I was looking at the photographs, and asking questions about them all as though they were long-lost relatives.

Anyway, I'll skip the gory bit, except to say I was really terrific, once I'd got her to talk herself into it. No simple job, I can tell you. It restored all my confidence in myself at one go, you could say. I couldn't help thinking of all the young birds who'd give anything to be in her shoes. Especially one who was back home with Auntie. And I must say she came up to scratch on the last lap. I had to get her to tone down her noises – I was afraid we'd have all the boarders coming down. I mean the moans that came off of her lips were out of this world. Guess what she came out with when it was all over: "Not the first time you've done that," she said. Then she told me a sweet little fact – she told me it was the first time in all her life it had "gone right for her" – as she put it. "At least I'll not go to my grave," she said, "wondering what it must be like." So there.

Here, why am I going on about her when I had this physiotherapist bint in mind?

I kept thinking it over, about that evening on the Downs, going over details closely, and this is the conclusion I came to. I decided she must have been a bit bent and didn't know it. And that it was that had put me off – because I'm very sensitive to any strong masculine touches in a woman. Some men like them, but to me they are out of place. After all, I had to think up something wrong with her – there couldn't be anything wrong with me, could there.

Now where was I? I seem to have side-tracked myself all over the show, and gone on to things not pertaining to what I had in mind to tell. Oh yes, I'm waiting for the lift in Thompson Court and I'm telling about remembering the first time I visited Ruby. I never finished that bit.

Something, I don't know what, had put me off my stroke. I mean before I'd even got started. I'd got myself invited and into her flat and now I was failing to make any impression at all. And I had this feeling that things were not well with me down below. I felt I'd got above myself, if you see what I mean, and I could see that she sensed what I was sensing about myself. I mean, I suddenly got a strong notion that she was dead uninterested in me, and had decided she'd been overseen in me at the start. Matter of fact, now that I'm beginning to think of it again, I do believe I've struck on what it was caused the mishap of feeling (if you'll only keep rooting round a thing the facts underneath it will usually come to the surface).

It was the following: now you know how it is when you begin to mix with people who are above your station. They like to lead you on, and draw you out; only to slap you down when it suits them. I mean they've been lapping it all up when suddenly you spot their face changing – then they start telling you they've heard enough. SO I think I'll play it reserved, play it dead cool with Ruby. The only trouble was I overplayed my hand, and instead of being cool I finds myself frozen, if you get me. All the power gone out of me, to put it another way. Right, so the batteries have run out. We're both standing there and there's not even a spark. So what do I do? I start off insulting her.

I went on about the flats first, how the tenants were like rats in a cage, and then I picked on one or two things she had, said she went in a lot for knick-knackery and all that stuff. I mean you can accuse a woman of anything, but never tell her she's got bad taste. Especially if she comes from a better station. There was one danger that she might cock a deaf'un and take no notice. But she didn't. That would have caused a dead flop. No, she began to get riled. So then I begin to come out with all the four-letter words, as they refer to them, which I wouldn't normally do to a woman who owns three hairdressers' shops. So she said: "I think you'd better go." Not that she minded the words – it was the way I was using them.

She looked at me like she hated my guts. Well a woman who hates you *might* let you, but a woman who isn't interested just doesn't want to know. At least you've got a spark in the fire, even if it might burn the bloody house down. "Yes, the sooner the better – " I said. So just as I'm going out I suddenly turn round and kiss her. I mean *kiss*. And I whisper a mouthful of dead naughty things into her ear – but very gentle this time. Know what, she turned to clay in my hands.

You can swing it from hate to love much quicker than from what they call indifference to love, if you follow me. And you'll feel better in yourself for having got something off your mind. Women don't really mind being insulted all that much – what gets on their wick is always being taken for granted. Course it don't work with every woman. Don't get that idea. It don't work with slow thinkers. They're still in that temper zone when you've moved over to the love zone. And it don't work with excitable women. They boil over and there's nothing left in the pot for love.

I stood on this red carpet outside the door and I rang the bell. Yes, finally, those two old crows got out of the lift and let it go. For a minute I got a little sinking feeling in case Ruby might be out, but I listened against the door and I could just hear the sound of the radio on. I felt a right ponce, standing there holding this bunch of flowers, so when she didn't open the door at once I gave the bell a long ring so that she'd know certain for sure it was me. The next thing I hear her voice from behind the door.

"Who is it?" she called out.

Not "Is that you, Alfie?" but "Who is it?" "It's me, Rube," I called. "I thought I'd give you a surprise visit."

"Alfie!" she said. "You couldn't have come at a worse time. I've got one of my headaches."

Now if there's one thing I do detest it's a woman who suffers from headaches – I mean a lot. I mean whilst she's got the headache. It's something they should keep to themselves. Not that Ruby had many. In fact, this was the first so far as I was concerned.

"Well open the bloody door," I said.

"I tell you I'm no use to anybody," she said. But she opened the door. She was wearing a dressing-gown and I could see she'd nothing on underneath. Her hair was all over the place, and to be quite frank, she wasn't exactly the picture I'd been painting in my mind of her. To come out straight, she looked dead blowsy. Not that I minded; I've got a weakness for blowsy women. They seem to be living in a more natural state.

"Oh hello, Alfie," she said. "I thought you said you were going to Ascot. I've a terrible attack of migraine. My poor head is splitting."

"Don't worry, gal," I said. "I'm not coming in, just brought you these." And I handed her the flowers.

She took them with a look of surprise, pulled the paper away, and looked at them, and her whole face changed in front of my eyes. "Oh what a nice thought!" she said, "but they're beautiful!" It seems she can't believe her own eyes. Funny how birds love flowers. I wouldn't give a thank-you if they brought me Kew Gardens in a basket.

"You take a few Aspros, gal," I said, "and rest yourself in a dark room with a cold wet cloth over your eyes. That's the answer for that little lot."

"I will," she said. "Oh thanks, Alfie," and she leant forward and gave me a little kiss on the lips. "I never thought I'd live to see the day," she whispered, and her little eyes were full of promise for the future when her headache would have gone.

"You live an' learn," I said. "Well, so long, Rube," I had a feeling I didn't want to hang about. In fact I could feel the little man on my shoulder urging me to scarper.

"Goodbye, Alfie," she said. "Give me a ring tomorrow. I'll be all right then."

"Sure," I said. "We might have an early session." Just as she's closing the door a thought struck me. "Here, Rube," I said, "you haven't twenty-five quid handy, have you?"

"Twenty-five pounds!" she said.

"Forget it," I said. If there's one thing I can't bear it's asking them for something and seeing them hesitate. I mean it's bad enough having to ask.

"Don't get huffy," she said. "Do you need it badly?"

"I need it," I said, "– or I wouldn't ask. But not all that badly. It's only till tomorrow."

"Wait there," she said. "I'll get it. I'll not be a tick."

I grabbed her wrist: "Don't think that was why I brought you the roses –" I said.

"I never gave it a thought," she said.

"A pony is neither here nor there to me," I said. "It's just that I want to give somebody something – and if I don't do it today I'll never do it."

"I understand," she said. "Wait there –"

I got hold of her arm again: "Listen Rube," I said, "I've got something important I'd like to talk over with you soon. But not whilst you've a headache."

"I see," she said. She looked at the roses: "They are lovely. I'll not be a tick. Oh my head –" She went in and I thought to myself: she's a good sort is Rube. Yes, I'll definitely settle down with her one way or another. Sunday noons, wearing one of these foulard silk neckerchiefs under an opennecked Viyella shirt, cavalry twill trousers – or a nice Cheviot or grey Saxony – and a pair of Tricker's benchmade suede shoes, handing out the gin cocktails and Manhattans to the guests. I'll bet I could get away with it. I'd just have to polish up the old chat a bit – nothing more.

CHAPTER THIRTY

JUST then I heard the lift stopping, and as I didn't want to be seen standing there in the corridor, I just nudged myself inside the door. I could see Ruby in the bedroom looking in a drawer. Then the next thing I saw another door opening. It was the bathroom. That's funny, I thought. Then I saw one bloke come out. He was a big geezer, and he had one of Ruby's coloured bath towels all round him. He was all steaming like he's just got out of the bath. There was something what they call familiar about him, but I couldn't just place him at once.

"Is that you, Alfie?" he said.

Big Lofty! I'd never noticed what enormous broad shoulders he had, and his hair was all curly being wet.

"Hy, Lofty," I said.

"How're things?" he said.

"Not bad," I said. "Not bad at all. The United are not doing as well this season." Knowing he came from near Manchester and was a keen supporter I thought I'd take a dig. I could have come across with a better stroke – if I'd had my wits about me. I think I set him back a bit – I mean turned his mind to football.

Ruby came slowly out of the bedroom with the notes in her hand. I suppose she thought it was no use hurrying now the damage was done. She looked at Lofty as though she'd like to crown him. But in a way I suppose I was the one to blame for going inside. That's a slip you should never make. Always leave a bird a way out. Come to think of it I must have sensed it all along. A man's feelings are often sharper than his mind.

"Who told you to come out?" she said.

"I told myself," he said.

"Well, tell yourself to get back in," she said, "– you great big ugly nit."

"I got tired of waiting in the bath for you, Ruby," he said. He'd put that one in for me.

"Shut your effin' mouth," she said. "And get back inside. Don't stand there – you're ruining my carpet." She turned to me: "I'm sorry, Alfie – I can't tell you how sorry I am," she said.

"Do me a favour!" I said. "You don't think I didn't know!"

She made to slip me the money but I didn't take it. Same as I say, I didn't have my wits about me.

"You're not going off, Alfie, are you?" said Lofty.

"I thought I would be," I said. I felt a bit leaden in the feet though. It seemed I couldn't get moving.

Now he had started off putting the knife in; he'd come out of the bathroom for that purpose, but half-way through his act it seems his feelings or something have suffered a change.

"Come on inside, mate," he said. "I know exactly how it feels. You must know that."

I saw him come towards me. I never realised he was that big. I always feel there's something just that bit horrible about big men, as though their glands or something have got out of hand. Or perhaps it's my imagination. They can't have much sense – not and grow that size. You've either got to run for it, I told myself, or else there'll be only one other thing: you'll have to kick him in the cobblers. Now I don't mind running – but this time I didn't. Old Lofty had his arm out and I told myself: it's now or never! When just then I spotted the look in his eyes. He wasn't after me to get me. He felt sorry for me!

"Don't take it like that, Alfie," he said. "What's done is forgotten. Come on in – there's enough for both of us. Enough of everything." And he patted old Ruby on the backside.

Know what, he carried it off without it looking the least bit kinky. I saw from the new look on Ruby's face that she wouldn't mind if I did go in and we all had a session. Just for the moment I'll admit I was tempted. It's always nicer to join in than go off on your own. But on second thoughts I decided not. I wondered in my mind could he be just a bit bent. I don't know what it is about me, but anything like that seems to put me right off.

172

"Sorry, Lofty," I said, "but I've got to be going. As a matter of fact I have other fish to fry."

"Alfie," said Ruby, coming right up to me, "you know how it is. He told me about this Annie. Now what else had you to tell me?"

I couldn't think of an answer just then, so I gave her the old Victory sign, although I was sorry as soon as my fingers went up. Why should I do a thing like that? Then off I went along the corridor. I don't know what they clean the carpets with but they seem to smell of shaving cream. Coming down in the lift I thought to myself: you know what you are, Alfie, you're a right bleeding innocent.

CHAPTER THIRTY-ONE

I MUST have got back to my place towards six o'clock. The streets seemed suddenly to be dead quiet, except for some church bells that were pealing out. I went in and I tiptoed up the stairs to my drum. I didn't want to be seen or heard. Now when I opened the door inside was all so silent and still, and it was going a bit darkish, and I caught this faint smell of Dettol, and of blood or something, that the first thought that crossed my mind was that something had gone wrong and Lily had snuffed it.

I was thankful to see she hadn't. She was lying stretched out there on the sofa, and her eyes were closed. And to be quite frank, you could have even took her for dead then. She wasn't sleeping or anything and she wasn't making any sound, she was just lying there, and when I went across the room to her she just opened her eyes and looked up at me. She didn't say anything. She didn't even look as though she hated me, or had anything against me, for how I'd gone off and left her. She just looked at me as though I was something and nothing. It seemed an effort even to lift her eyelids. Then she slowly closed them again, just like that. I could see at a glance it was all over. The look on her face was quite different. In fact I could sense it in the air, if you see what I mean. Still, I had to make sure. And you've got to say something.

"Everything all right now?" I said.

"Everything all right?" she said. "Yes, everything's all right." She hesitated and then she tried to rise: "I must get up," she said. "There's something I didn't do. I must do it now."

"Hold on a minute, gal," I said, "I'll make you a cup of char first. I expect you could do with one." I mean she looked so white, her skin so waxy, and somehow she seemed to have lost a lot of weight. I'd never given it a thought that a thing like that would knock so much out of a woman.

"No, don't!" she said. I was taken aback to hear her speak so sharp, and so loud. "I don't want you to –".

"O.K.," I said. "O.K. I won't bother." I mean if they won't accept a kindness it doesn't do to force it on them. As I made for the kitchen – I thought I'd have a good wash and freshen up – she got up.

"Don't go in there," she said.

"Why not?" I said. "What's up?"

"I don't want you to go in," she said.

"Why not?" I said.

"I have some cleaning up to do," she said. "Don't go in."

"You leave it all to me, gal," I said, "it's no trouble."

After all, what was there to it, a little bit of mopping up. And she looked as though she hadn't the strength to bend down. For the minute I thought she was going to jump up and stop me. Then it seemed she came over faint or something because she rested herself back on the sofa. She may have had a change of mind, for she spoke as if she couldn't care less, and anything I did was on my own head.

"Right, go in then," she said, "if you must."

She kept her eyes on me. I went in where it must all have happened to her. And I closed the door behind me.

CHAPTER THIRTY-TWO

Now, I've gone into that room, and things don't seem so bad there. Well, the one first thought behind my mind was that I didn't want any evidence left lying round. I suppose it was fear – fear for my own skin. Do a job yourself and you know it's done well. Then suddenly I've seen something and I've had the shock of my life. I mean I've come upon this *thing*, – I mean, this child. I don't care what anybody says, that's what it was. It was so small, yet so real, see, not fully grown, yet so beautifully shaped, and so human. All I was expecting to see – well I don't rightly know what I was expecting – but certainly not this perfectly formed little being – this infant. Nobody had ever told me about those things. I had to stoop down and pick it up, see, for it was lying on this little white napkin where Lily had put it. And as I brought it up under my gaze I half expected it to cry out. It was so identical to a living baby. It didn't cry out of course – it couldn't have done, it could never had had life in it. I mean proper separate life of its own. It must have had some life, the life God gave it, see. And the way it lay there, so silent, so still, quite touched me. I thought *"I'm your Dad."* Now it's strange I should think a thing like that at a time like that, but it's exactly what I did think. I held him in my hands, see, and I had this feeling: *"This is my son, and I'm one of them that has done this to him."* And the more it comes to me that he's dead, and will never breathe the breath of life again, the closer he feels to me as my son, if you see what I mean.

Now after that first shock, I had this job to do, of getting rid of it. I didn't want to – Oh Jesus, I didn't want! – but I *had* to. I had no choice. This is what life does to you, I'm thinking, it forces you into a corner, and you've got to do things you don't want to do. Now as I'm doing it, forcing myself to get rid of this innocent little thing, I start praying or something. Just letting words come off my tongue. And I could hear myself saying, *"Christ, help me"* and things like that, and the next thing I'm crying. Straight up, tears are rushing out of my eyes, and running down my face. I'd forgot how salty tears taste when they pour out of you. Not for him I wasn't crying. Nah, he was past it. I was crying for my poor bleeding self. I felt that lost and helpless all of a sudden, see. I'll tell you one thing – it don't half bring it home to you what you are and what you have done when you see a helpless little thing like that lying in front of you in your own hands. You try to tell yourself that it's happening all over the world – that it happens at some time or other to everybody – but somehow talk don't work at that moment.

Then I think how he had been quite perfect, and the thought crossed my mind: "*You know what you did, Alfie, you murdered him.*" I mean what a stroke for the mind to come out with, a thing like that. "*Yes, mate, you set it all up and for thirty nicker you had him done to death.*" And then it struck me that the main idea in my head had been how to get it done a fiver cheaper. That's all I'd been thinking of when Lily arrived.

Now I find I can't get that thought out of my mind – how I had fixed it up to have him done to death. So then I've gone and put my head under the cold water tap. I thought where the tears had been wouldn't show if I did that. And I had a good wash with carbolic soap to freshen up. Then at last, when I've got control of myself, and I've swallowed everything down, I mean all the thoughts and feelings and things, the lot, and I'm just finishing drying myself off, a funny thing happened.

You know how you sometimes hear sounds, and you take no notice of them – well I can hear *a little baby crying*. So I stop and listen, and sure enough, no mistake, I could hear this crying. Quite distinct it was. Well, there was no kid in sight anywhere, and there's no infant in the house, so I reckoned it couldn't have been a child. But I stood there and listened, and on and on it went. I thought it might have been the wind outside, see, moaning or something, you know the way it does. But there was no wind. But I shut the window tight to keep it out and make sure. But that didn't stop it. Then it struck me it could be the water in the pipes. You often get those things making noises. So I shut the tap off dead hard to be certain. Yet it still kept on in my ear, this baby crying. So I decided it must be the imagination, and on and on it went, wailing and wailing away, as if it would go on wailing to the end of my days.

CHAPTER THIRTY-THREE

I DECIDED to give myself a complete change; fresh shirt, socks, trunks, suit, shoes, the lot. In fact I put on my light-weight flannel trousers and dark blazer, which I hadn't worn for a bit. I find I'm very influenced by what I'm wearing at any one time, and I thought if I dressed casual I might begin to feel more light hearted or something. It might have struck Lily that I was a long time tidying up, but she seemed to be lying in a faint doze on the sofa. She was miles away, you could say. Now as luck would have it I find I have a tin of Sainsbury's pure coffee in, flavour sealed, one that Annie must have stored away. So I opened it, and I make a big jug full of coffee. Then I went in to her and tapped her on the shoulder, and showed her I was looking all bright and chipper. Never let a woman see what you've gone through. Well, I mean, they might feel *sorry* for you.

"Here y'are, gal," I said. "There's a nice cup of coffee for you, the real thing. I've put the top of the milk in for you, and I bet you wouldn't get a better cup no matter where you went."

I think the real secret is to use plenty of coffee, have the jug hot, and see that the water is on the sizzle as it's going in. I was afraid for the minute she might say: "No thanks." That would have spoilt everything, but she didn't. I kept on chatting her up as she was drinking it about how a man will always make better tea or coffee than a woman because he's got more patience. Same as I say, you've got to say something. And I find I'm very good on those little tactics. She didn't speak, and she didn't not speak, if you follow me, but she looked a lot better after she'd drunk it. A little tinge of colour started coming to her cheeks.

"Now, if you're ready, Lily," I said, "I can run you all the way back home."

"I'd sooner go alone," she said. She was quite flat about that.

"Suits me," I said, "if you'd sooner go on your tod. You can get a train from Waterloo, or there's a Green Line bus will run all the way. I'm not sure of the times."

"I know the way," she said. "I'll get home all right. Don't worry."

She put on her coat. I didn't like to see her going off like that, but it's a mistake to press a woman against her will. "Here y'are," I said. "Don't forget your basket." I picked up her basket and we both looked into it and saw the same thing – the squiggly letter the kid had written to his Dad. Now when I saw that a funny thought struck me.

"Just a tick, Lily," I said, "I knew there was something."

She stood there near the door wondering what the something could be. You can always catch a woman with curiosity. I went to the wardrobe, and felt on top at the back. I was afraid for a minute that it might have been knocked off, but it hadn't. I got out this large brown bag. Yes, it was quite safe. Never been opened for years. Never been touched, never been looked at.

"Here y'are," I said to her. "You can take this home for young Phil. Mind, the bag handle's got broke."

"For who?" she said, staring at me.

"Young Phil," I said. "Your youngest kid what writes these funny letters to his Dad."

"I didn't know you knew," she said.

"I know a lot more than you think," I said. "I bought this for a kid I used to know – but somehow I never got round to giving it him."

She stood there and seemed to be in two minds about taking the parcel off of me.

"What is it?" she said.

"Would you like to see it?" I said.

I put my hand inside this brown bag and take out this marvellous Teddy bear that I'd bought for Malcolm on that Saturday morning a long time ago. Wasn't it strange, though, how he didn't even know his own father? There was more truth than I'd imagined in what I told old Harry about the way kids forget. You try to teach somebody something and ten to one the lesson of it will come home to you first.

Without thinking I took out the Teddy bear, held it up and then threw it across to Lily. It went flying through the air and she made a grab with her two hands held upwards as though she was catching a child. She held it still for a second or two up in the air, then pulled it down to herself. Just then it let out a tiny little squeak. I'd forgot it had this squeak built in. Know what, that sound went right through me.

Anyway, I see she's standing there a-holding this Teddy bear in her arms and looking in a real daze. So I put my arm round her shoulders. I mean I couldn't have let her go home on her own in that state. She might have been knocked down. Then there would have been questions asked. So I said: "Come on Lily, I will run you home after all. You tell him it's from his Uncle Donald."

So Lily turns to me and puts her face right up against my chest. Pressed it into me. Somehow I thought that was what you call a friendly gesture. Forgiving you might say. So I patted her little back, what seemed to have got stooped like she was a lot older than her years.

"Come on, mate," I said. "The kids will be waiting for you."

CHAPTER THIRTY-FOUR

I GOT Lily seated in the car. "I'll not be a minute," I said, "there's something I have to pick up." She nodded and sat there with the Teddy on her knee. I slipped in next door to Sharpey. He was watching the box. "You ain't got a pony handy?" I said. He put his hand in his fob pocket, took out a little roll and peeled me five fivers off. "See you," I said. "Take care of yourself," he said. A good mate Sharpey. You can't have everything.

It was funny that drive down to Maidenhead. I don't think we spoke more than two words, yet it was real understanding all the way. Never attempt to make out what you're not to a bird – because what you are is bound to come out sooner or later. And it's that that she can get hold of. That's why women often prefer a villain to the average man – at least they know what he is.

Lily just sat there looking straight in front of her. And for some reason best known to herself she would keep that Teddy bear on her knee. Of course, same as I say, it was a real beauty, this lovely nylon fur, and the woman who made it had struck it off to perfection. I had a funny thought kept coming to me – that in a way I'd been as close to Lily as old Harry had ever been. Not as close as husband and wife are, in their kids and their chat about families and all that, but as close inside as a man and woman are likely to get in this life. And I don't mean the little kefuffle on the river bank. I mean that little moment when I flung her the bear and she came and leant up against me. You get closer in pain than in pleasure.

So there we are driving along this new road they've built, and I'm thinking how old Harry will one day come out of the sanatorium, and they'll start their little life again, at home, with the three kids, and she'll have to go about her daily routine, and they'll eat together and chat together and watch the telly in the evenings, and put the kids to bed together, and have a little talk about the future, about the kids' education, the price of meat and the winter sales, and then they'll go to bed themselves, and old Harry might perform or he might not, and he'll lie there beside her and he'll think, if he thinks at all, it's my little Lily who I know inside out, and then he'll drop off to sleep content, and little Lily might drop off, or she might have one last memory and thought in her mind, about this day that's just gone, and come to that, she might even remember our little three-minute fling that Sunday beside the bank of the Thames, since if you work it out, one goes with the other. It must be dead funny the things that go on in a bird's mind as she lies there next to her old man at night. Yet it must happen to all of us at some time.

Now the odd thing is this – you might think a thing like that would come between husband and wife. I don't think so. I think if they love each other it could bring them closer together. I'll bet when she has that thought she won't turn away from old Harry. She'll turn towards him and put her arm round him and he'll think: Blimey, old Lil's got one of her lovey moods on her tonight.

As she was getting out of the car I gave her a kiss on the cheek, and slipped the five fivers into her pocket. I done it so nice, see, I couldn't help admiring myself as I drove off: *Alfie*, I thought, *you're quite the little gentleman* – in your own way, that is. It's a cosy little feeling to get now and again is that, though it wouldn't do for regular. I expect it would work out too expensive in the long run – for what you'd get out of it, if you see what I mean.

CHAPTER THIRTY-FIVE

THE trouble in this world is that you've got nobody to talk to. People only hold it against you, what you tell them. I was longing to find somebody, a mate or even a bird, that I could talk to about the things that had happened to me that day. I think your life only starts sorting itself out once you begin to have a good rabbit about it and put it into words; on top of which look what you get off your chest at the same time. Now for a talk like that to come off you've got to have a good listener – and it can either be a good mate or a complete stranger. If it's a stranger, it's got to be somebody you'll never meet again, and if it's a mate, he's got to be prepared to forget the whole thing once you've told him. You don't want him to keep bringing it up. You only tell him to shift the load. You don't want to take it back again. But somehow in these days nobody seems to want to listen. I suppose what it amounts to, they've all got troubles enough of their own. Not only that, but when you get down to it we never listen to anybody but ourselves. Leastways, I hardly ever do. Course, had I told Sharpey and Perce I know exactly what they would have said: *All right,* they'd say, *you put her up the club – but she asked for it – and you behaved real decent, didn't you, you helped her out. What more can a man do?* It's exactly what I'd have said myself if it had happened to some other geezer instead of me. But when it happens you, you get to know things they can never know.

Now about nine o'clock that same evening, I've driven back to London but I find I can't face going into my own gaff. Not alone. I've still got the memory of this little dead thing on my mind. Well, not the memory – I've more or less buried that when I buried him – but I've got this dark little lump of cold grief or something settled over my heart. It could, of course, be wind, since I've hardly eaten all day. Just the same, I reckon it'll take a bleeding good Maclean's powder to move that little lot.

Now I didn't want to wander back onto my own stamping ground in case I should run into Sharpey or Perce or any other mate, so I just stop the car on the Embankment, just there opposite Scotland Yard, where you can look across the river to the County Hall, the Festival Hall and all that other stuff they've put up there. So I lean over the Embankment wall and look down at the Thames that's going out. I find it very soothing to the eyes seeing that water flow by. Apart from the load of rotten rubber goods that go floating by, sometimes you'll see as many as a dozen, the odd one about a foot long, slipping by like a narrow gutted ghost, all that's left from some young couple's minute or two of sealed off passion. It makes you think. And whilst I'm looking down at these and other little signs of London life going by, the odd dead cat and so forth, I begin to realise a very funny thing: *I have that Ruby behind my mind.*

Now who'd have thought a great big lustbox like that would worm her way into a man's feelings – let alone mine! Thinking it over, however, whilst she might have looked a hard case to some, that was only a front, and underneath, when you got a glimpse of it, she could be real mumsie. And same as I say, she was in beautiful condition. And that's not a thing to be sneezed at in these days. They don't come riper than Ruby. Know what, I'm beginning to think she *was* beautiful. I mean it's not in the eyes you see beauty, it's in the hunger of your poor bloody heart. If that's not coming it too strong.

Then I begin to wonder is this love lark really worth it. I mean, when I look back on my little life, and I think of the birds I've known, and of all each one of those little birds has done for me, and of how little I've ever done for them – yet they couldn't have cost me more or took more out of me if I'd given them everything I had. That's the rub. The feelings have got to be drawn out of you one way or another, so it's as well to hold nothing back at the start. With birds it's as well to give – give – give; it'll work out cheaper in the long run.

As I was standing there I looked up and there I saw one geezer coming along eyeing me, and as he got nearer I thought – poor old sod, he's queer, and then the thought half struck me as he went by, looking a bit sad like some of them do, like they were always on the lookout for something they know they'll never find, and if they do find it they know it won't last; and same as I say, the thought went through my mind how many a young bloke like me might *go over*, if you see what I mean, and look round for one of these bent old boys who was rich, and who would take him in, give him a home, buy him his gear over in Jermyn Street or somewhere, shirts made to measure and all that caper, and make a fuss of him, perhaps set him up as his chauffeur, and see he was never short of a tenner, and at the same time relieve him of his responsibilities. Not that you have that many if you're like me. I mean it looks such an easy number for any goodlooking young layabout a life like that, that I'm only surprised more don't go in for it. Mind you, for a start you've got to be a bit bent yourself underneath to take up that way of living, otherwise just imagine how horrible it must be at certain times. Another snag is this – if a bloke's queer it's odds-on he'll hate parting with money. It's not only that they don't like parting, but into the bargain they want to have you around, and to keep you on a string. They work it out that the more they give you the less dependent on them you are. Leastways that's been my experience – such as it's been. And it's a dead cert that the odd queer who has a generous heart will already have been lapped up by some young villain, and will have been turned over more than once.

So I put that thought aside, and I think to myself, as I lean over the Embankment wall and watch old Father Thames steaming by, *look at me now!* I've got some money, haven't I, and I've got a few good suits, a fair car, and I've got my health back. But I haven't got *my peace of mind. And if you haven't got that you've got nothing!*

There's one certainty: I'll go no more a-birding. I suppose I've just got to sweat this little lot out of me one way or another – what they call suffer it through. But what's the answer? That's what I keep asking myself. I suppose it's what everybody in this life is asking themselves.

CHAPTER THIRTY-SIX

THOSE sort of feelings about is-your-life-worthwhile don't half knock it out of you. They're worse than a day's graft. Especially if you're not in training for them. So what do I decide to do but cross the frog and slip into a pub down a side street opposite the House of Commons. Now, I'm just having this quiet drink, a Worthington as a matter of fact, which I don't like the taste of all that much, but being Sunday I didn't want to pint it, and it is a strong drink, and somehow it always do make the bloke behind the bar look up a bit when you order one of them, leastways that's the impression I've got. Now let me see how it was. Yes, I'm drinking this when I spot a woman's back in a little cubby recess at the side. I know those shoulders, I think; I look a bit closer and guess what – it's only Siddie!

She's sitting there on her jacksie, reading one of these colour things out of a newspaper – the *Sunday Times* Supplement or whatever they call it. It's got one geezer on the cover with a stocking over his face. I can't understand why she hasn't got a bloke in tow. So I creep up close, don't I, and stoop and whisper into her ear: "Suck one of these mints, Siddie, so he don't smell your breath!"

She turned and stared up at me like I was a ghost from

the past. That's the best I can put it. And once she's recognised me I can see from the look in her eyes that she's debating inside herself what line to take with me: the brush off or the half welcome. So I clinch it, don't I. "Siddie," I said, "you look marvellous! You look younger than ever. How do you do it? Cor, that's a lovely bit of Musquash –" and I stroke her coat. "Course you always was a snazzy dresser."

Naturally, in the middle of all this she comes out with something about: "Alfie, I wouldn't have known you!" But I decide to cock a deaf 'un to that. I mean I'm not sure how she intends it. So I ride it.

"What are you having?" I said. "The usual – vodka and tomato juice?"

"I'm waiting for somebody," she said.

"Yes," I said, "and he's arrived."

"He hasn't," she said. "He's a buyer from the firm."

"You were never one to wait for a man, Siddie," I said.

"I waited long enough for you," she said.

"I can explain all that," I said. "On my solemn oath if I were to die this minute," I was going to say *tonight* instead of *this minute,* and whether it is I'm getting religious or not I don't know, but I felt I didn't want a threat like that hanging over my head for more than the next sixty seconds. "Come on, drink up. We'd better be off before this buying geezer arrives."

When I looked closer at her face it did seem that bit worn, but her chest was as beautiful as ever. I believe they can actually improve with age if given proper attention. The cleavage if anything was better. From the little I saw of it. Same as I say, I was leaning over her.

"I'm not sure," she said. "I'm not at all sure." She had a look towards the door.

"You look in need of a good laugh, gal," I said. "Laughter keeps a woman young, don't forget."

"Have you got your napkin?" she said.

"I'm like the Boy Scouts," I said – "always prepared." And I found myself whipping out my one spotless hanky which I'd resisted blowing my nose on and I tucked it over my lapel. "What time did your old man say he'd be waiting for you at the station?"

"He's gone to Perth on his job," she said, half rising from her seat. "He won't be back until Tuesday morning."

"Then I won't need my napkin," I said. "I never wear 'em in bed. Come on, I've got the car waiting round the corner." So she got up, didn't she, and I've put my arm in hers and led her outside.

It felt so soft, so warm and cosy under her armpit up against her breast. There's no doubt that few things in this life are more comforting to have your mitt tucked away in than a woman's plump arm inside a fur coat, even though it might only be dyed Musquash. It reminds me of a bird I once knew who used to like to – but why tell it? People don't respect you more for opening your heart to them and telling all the things you've done. I think you're only making a stick for your own back. Anyway, you only remind them of what they've done but not told. It gives them a guilty feeling. Nobody is going to thank you for *that*.

Well, I'd had a good cleansing out, and now I felt badly in need of a good filling up again. As we walked along the pavement towards Westminster Bridge I couldn't believe how all this weight had suddenly lifted off my heart. It's funny, I thought, but all that pain and sorrow don't last all that long. I don't suppose anything does. Forgive yourself, Alfie, I said, for anything you've done wrong. After all, you've got to forgive yourself before you can forgive anybody else, if you see what I mean.

"Remember that time you got your knee stuck on the horn?" I said.

Come to think of it, that was when it all started. That was the selfsame night when little Gilda was overdue. Quite a bit had happened in between.

Siddie let out one of her hearty laughs. Same as I say, she's got these powerful lungs. I find I'm going in more for healthy women.

"You never change – do you, Alfie?" she said.

I dodged that one: "It's all a giggle, Siddie," I said. And as I opened the car door for her I gave her behind such a nice little pat. Then I goes round and gets into the driver's seat, and drives off, all smiles. And I think to myself: *Alfie, you're a real little Punchinello.*

Well, you've got to be in this life, if you see what I mean.